WILD BLUE

TYSON WILD BOOK THIRTY FOUR

TRIPP ELLIS

"Just because the guy runs funny doesn't mean he's a killer," Sheriff Daniels said.

"It's him," I replied with conviction.

The sheriff's skeptical eyes surveyed me. "You sure?"

"I chased him halfway across campus. I'm pretty damn sure."

I could understand his hesitancy. My face was still stained with the remnants of clown makeup, and the temporary green hair dye was still doing its thing. I looked like something the cat dragged in, still wearing my costume from the night before—a purple suit, orange vest, green shirt, and tie. The night before involved copious amounts of alcohol as well as a delightful young lady. I hadn't been home to change yet. I came straight from campus after taking Amethyst back to her hotel.

The horror convention was over, and she and Ophelia were catching a flight out this afternoon. It was a fun adventure while it lasted. We had said our goodbyes and promised to keep in touch. The horror convention would be back in town next year, and I figured she might be as well.

The bustle of activity filled the Sheriff's Department, and the midmorning sun filtered through the blinds. Motes of dust floated in the slashes of light. Fingers clacked against keyboards, phones rang, and the smell of fresh coffee filled the air.

"I can't get a warrant because the guy has a funny gait," the sheriff said. "Get something substantial."

"I will," I said before ambling to the coffee pot and pouring myself a cup. At least this time of the morning it was fresh.

I mixed in cream and sugar, then made my way to Denise's desk. She had an amused look on her face as her emerald eyes surveyed my disheveled appearance. "Rough night?"

"Adventurous," I said with a grin.

"What was her name?"

Denise knew me all too well. "Amethyst."

"The psychic?" she said with a disapproving arch of her brow.

"Medium. Not psychic."

She rolled her eyes.

"You want a cup of coffee?" I asked, changing the subject.

"No, thank you. Did you hear about the shark attack?"

I lifted a surprised brow. "There was another one?"

"Snorkeler on one of the reefs. Bull shark took a chunk out of his leg. He was rushed to the emergency room. Listed in critical but stable condition. Now there's a bunch of folks out on the water hunting the shark, and Daniels is a little concerned that things are going to get out of hand."

"Isn't shark finning illegal now?"

"I don't think these would-be hunters are concerned with the fins. The victim's wife put up a bounty for whoever brings in the shark that bit her husband."

"How would they know if they got the right shark?"

Denise shrugged.

"There's a bull shark limit of 1 per day."

"I don't think these people are going to abide by limits. I think it's terrible all the way around, but hunting every shark around the island isn't an appropriate solution. Sharks are a vital part of the ecosystem. They keep things in check."

"Well, hopefully, common sense prevails."

Denise scoffed. "Common sense isn't always that common."

She wouldn't get much argument from me on that point.

"Where's your partner in crime?" she asked.

"I'm not exactly sure. We got separated last night."

"I'm sure he'll have a story to tell," Denise said.

I grinned. "I'm sure he will. What about you? How was your Halloween?"

"My Halloween was rather low-key. I went with a girlfriend to a costume party, then I came home and watched a bunch of scary movies, then proceeded to have nightmares all night. I don't know why I do that to myself, but there is something fun about watching a spooky movie alone in the dark."

"I can't imagine that you would ever have to spend a night alone."

She smirked. "By choice. I have high standards. And some people aren't emotionally available," she taunted.

I arched an eyebrow at her.

My phone buzzed with a call from JD. "Speak of the devil."

I took the call and held the phone to my ear.

"You are not going to believe this," JD said.

"Where are you?"

"I just dropped Ophelia off at the hotel. Have I got a story for you."

"I'm sure. Pick me up at the station. I think I know who the campus killer is."

Wind swirled about, and the Florida sun beamed down as we cruised back to *Diver Down* in JD's Miami Blue Porsche.

Jack was showered, clean-shaven, and had on a fresh set of clothes—his typical uniform of a Hawaiian shirt, cargo shorts, and checkered Vans. It was clear he actually made it home last night and didn't spend the evening under the stars like I had done. With the top down and the stereo blasting, the wind tousled his long blond hair. Wearing classic Ray Bans and a satisfied smirk on his face, JD looked like he had a damn good time last night. He pestered me for the details of my adventure with Amethyst, then filled me in on his escapades with Ophelia.

"She wanted to go to the cemetery."

"Oh, no," I groaned. "Please tell me you didn't..."

"It was Halloween. She's a spooky girl." JD grinned.

"You didn't desecrate a grave with an unnatural act, did you?"

"There was nothing unnatural about it."

I gave him a look.

"No, of course not. We didn't desecrate a grave. I would never do something like that," JD said innocently. "We just took a moonlight stroll through the tombstones. Turns out we weren't the only people with that idea. You would be surprised at the number of idiots running around a cemetery after midnight on Halloween. It sure got her worked up, let me tell you. The moonlight, the eerie mist, the chirp of the crickets. We may or may not have gotten a little frisky in the car. I can neither confirm nor deny, mind you. But she gives great *headstone*. Just saying."

I rolled my eyes.

"I must admit, I'm a little sad to see her go," JD said. "We might have to make a road trip."

The girls lived in Los Angeles, and with Jack's daughter Scarlett topping the box office, we had plenty of excuses to get out to Tinseltown. LA was always an adventure of its own.

Scarlett's pursuit of the *acting thing* had turned her into a bona fide star almost overnight. *Ultra Mega 2* had spent the entire summer at #1 until it was knocked off by *Azagoth, Rise of the Damned*. Production would begin soon on *Ultra Mega 3*, and there was no sign that the franchise would slow down. There were lunch boxes, action figures, T-shirts, and Halloween costumes. I saw more than a few this season.

However, with David Cameron at the helm, the back-to-back filming of the series was delaying production on our TV show he was set to produce. It didn't really matter at this point. I'd already gotten paid for the story that was loosely based on some of our misadventures.

So far, Scarlett had been staying on the straight and narrow, but LA was a city full of temptation. Every vice was at your fingertips, and every celebrity had a crowd of *hanger-oners* that would enable their every whim. Stars became money machines for agents, managers, entertainment attorneys, and studios—*the suits*. Keep the machine rolling at all costs was their mantra.

Scarlett had her issues with substance abuse in the past, and I know a relapse was always on JD's mind. The nature of Scarlett's success put her in the fast lane. We both hoped it wasn't *too fast*. Fortunately, she had a great agent. Joel was one of the good guys in a town that could be less than angelic. He kept an eye on his star client, and Scarlett seemed largely unaffected by her newfound fame.

I filled Jack in on my theory about the campus killer as we drove across the island.

He flashed a skeptical glance in my direction. "Professor Matthews?"

"I'm telling you, he's the guy."

JD frowned. "That pompous little bastard? The one calling for more accountability from the Campus Police?"

"Yup."

"Figures." His face crinkled with disdain. "Let's go talk to the guy. Rattle his cage."

The engine howled, and the exhaust rumbled. We pulled into the lot at *Diver Down,* and JD drove around by the dock and found a place to park. We ambled to the *Avventura* and boarded the superyacht. Buddy greeted me in the salon with a wagging tail and a slobbering tongue.

JD took him out for a walk while I hustled up to my stateroom on the bridge deck, showered, and got changed. I grabbed my 9mm and holstered it in my waistband for an appendix carry. I shuffled down to the main deck and into the galley, where I began whipping up breakfast. Brunch, really.

I had scrambled eggs and fried bacon by the time JD returned, and we chowed before heading to find Professor Matthews.

I called Isabella, my handler at *Cobra Company,* on the drive and asked her to pull cell records for the professor. "See if you can put him at any of the crime scenes."

I gave her a list of times, incidents, and locations.

"I'll see what I can do."

I could have had Denise pull the records, but it would take a warrant and the cooperation of the phone company. Isabella could acquire the data much faster and without all the red tape. It wouldn't be admissible, but it would be a head start. I could always have Denise circle around and try to get the information legitimately.

Evan Matthews was a tenured professor at the prestigious university. He was known among students to be quite a hard-ass and unforgiving in both his grading and attendance policies. He loved to make an example of students that ran afoul of his authority. A little tyrant.

He lived in a bungalow on Stratton Avenue with a white picket fence, pastel yellow siding, white trim, and forest green doors and shutters. A large veranda wrapped around the home, and the yard was filled with tall palms. A cobblestone driveway led to the garage, and thick ivy wrapped around half of the picket fence.

It was a nice place. Tuition at Vanden wasn't cheap. By the looks of things, Professor Matthews drew a nice salary.

JD pulled to the curb, and we hopped out, pushed through the gate, and strolled the walkway to the veranda. We had both met Matthews during our previous investigation.

I banged on the door, and the professor answered a few minutes later. The flash of my badge didn't seem to dim his spirits.

"Good morning, Deputies. What can I do for you?"

He had the same build as the man I chased across campus. The same brown eyes. I only got a glimpse of them as they peered out behind a black ski mask during an attack. My blood boiled, and my blood pressure rose as I stared into his eyes, knowing he was responsible for at least one murder and several attempted assaults.

Even on his day off, Matthews wore a single-breasted brown tweed jacket and a pale blue Oxford shirt. His gold, wire-rimmed glasses circled his penny-brown eyes, and his wavy hair winged over his ears. He was mid 30s and had a pompous air about him. He looked down his nose at every-one, sure that his intellect was superior.

Matthews didn't seem to have a care in the world. His eyes flicked between the two of us with a smug look on his face.

"I saw you running around the track this morning," I said.

He gave me a curious look. "Yes, I try to get my miles in every day."

"Looks like you're having a little trouble with your hip. It's affecting your stride."

His brow knitted with confusion. "You're very observant, Deputy. Yes, my hip has been bothering me for about a month now. Maybe a little longer. My hip flexor is a little sore. I've been trying to stretch it out, but... I guess I'm just getting old." He chuckled. "Do you have an interest in sports medicine? Surely you didn't come here just to talk about my performance on the track?"

"I'm just here to ask you a few routine questions."

"Routine questions?" he mirrored suspiciously. "The *Campus Killer* I assume?"

I nodded.

"Or is it the *Coed Killer?*"

"I've heard both. Depends on which news channel you watch."

"I like Paris Delaney, personally. She's much more entertaining than that wannabe, Megyn Michaels."

"She has her qualities."

"I wish I could help you, but I wasn't anywhere near campus during those attacks. I didn't see anything."

"Can you tell me where you were during those incidents?"

His eyes narrowed, but he played it cool. "You're asking me questions like you consider me a suspect."

"Like I said, just routine."

"Just routine," he replied with thinly veiled skepticism. "Are you talking to all the male professors at the university?"

"Only the ones that match the perp's description."

"How much of a description can you have of a man that wears jeans, a black shirt, and a black ski mask?"

"The perp happens to be your height, build, and have your eye color."

"So do a lot of people. I'm all together average." It was an attempt at humility.

"The man I chased across campus had a hip flexor issue. It was obvious in his stride."

A wave of realization washed over him. "Ah, I see. My injury automatically makes me a suspect."

"Your injury makes you identifiable," I said pointedly.

"You're barking up the wrong tree, Deputies."

I rattled off the date and time of the first campus attack. "Eliza Parkes was assaulted between Brown and Duncan Hall. Where were you that night?"

4

Eliza was the first of several girls assaulted on campus, culminating with the brutal murder of Alison Christie.

"Like I said, I was nowhere near campus during those incidents," Professor Matthews said. "If you have any further questions, I suggest you contact my attorney. Good day, gentlemen."

He closed the door and latched it.

"He seems cooperative," JD muttered, his voice thick with sarcasm.

We spun around and ambled back down the walkway to the Porsche and climbed in. JD cranked up the engine and pulled away from the curb.

Isabella called me back. "Matthews was smart enough to leave his phone at home during all the attacks. Anything else on him?"

"Not at the moment."

"I did a little background on your person of interest. He's just a tad smarter than your average criminal. Got an IQ of 162, graduated from Vanden at the top of his class, and got his Ph.D. in molecular biology."

"No crime is perfect. Everybody makes mistakes. I'll get him," I vowed.

"You sure he's your guy?" Isabella asked. "His record is clean. No priors. I can't find any dirt on the guy."

"He's dirty, all right."

"I'll take your word for it. Let me know if you need anything else."

I thanked her and ended the call.

Daniels called as I slipped the phone back into my pocket. "I need you two nitwits to get over to the Aquarium."

"What's going on?"

"You'll see. Things keep getting weirder and weirder around here."

I ended the call and told JD to head to the Coconut Key Aquarium.

Built in the mid-40s, the Aquarium was open every day, seven days a week, from 10 AM to 6 PM. The tours featured talks on Atlantic game fish, sea turtles, shark feedings, and conservation, among other things.

Located on the northwest side of the island, the Aquarium was a massive structure on the wharf. Inside the white building with blue trim was an undersea world of adventure. Massive reproductions of Great Whites hung from the ceiling, bearing razor-sharp teeth. There were multiple pools of stingrays and other tropical fish. The walls were lined with giant aquariums filled with all kinds of marine life—jellyfish, alligators, isopods, clownfish, octopi, angelfish, dolphins, whales, eels, sea urchins, crabs, you name it. You could get up close and personal with the various creatures of the undersea domain. The Aquarium was also home to confiscated wildlife that was illegally harvested.

By far, the largest attraction was the sharks—a perennial favorite among children and adults. The deadly creatures of the deep provided endless fascination. Though, the apex predator of them all, the Great White, wouldn't be found in captivity. The savage creatures needed space to roam and feed. Despite their prowess, most died within weeks of captivity.

Great Whites may have stolen all the press and starred in all the movies, but it was the Bull Shark that was perhaps the more fearsome predator. With the strongest bite force of any shark species, and more shark attacks each year that any other species, the Bull Shark demanded respect. And the Coconut Key Aquarium was one of the few that had them on display.

They were plentiful in the surrounding waters and could often be seen around the reefs. They rarely caused trouble, and when they did, the bite was more out of curiosity than malice. Just their way of getting to know you. Humans aren't typically their preferred meal. They like fish, crustaceans, stingrays, seals, dolphins, even other small sharks. But hey, a snack is a snack.

The main attraction was the domed aquarium. A marvel of engineering. The new exhibit had been added a few years ago. Walking into the room was like standing at the bottom of the ocean. An immersive experience with a 200° window into the aquatic world. Sharks finned about, prowling their domain with cold, callous eyes.

The incident had caused the Aquarium to shut down for the rest of the day. All of the patrons had been ushered out and given a raincheck or refund. We flashed our badges at the main entrance and were quickly greeted by the general manager.

Claire Fortier was in her mid 40s with short blonde hair that fell past her ears and bangs that hung just above her overly sculpted brows. The short cut framed her boxy face well.

We made introductions, and she escorted us through the facility. "I have to warn you, it's disturbing."

5

"We recently acquired a bull shark," Claire said. "It was caught in a fishing net and was wounded. We've been nursing it back to health. It was behaving oddly and not eating. We feared it might not make it. Then it coughed up this," she said, pointing to a ragged, decomposing leg laying on the floor.

Still wet and surrounded by speckles of water, the appendage had been severed at the calf. The foot and ankle were completely intact, and there was a small, glittering silver ankle bracelet. Pink manicured toenails adorned the petite foot, and a red rose was tattooed on the dorsal side of the foot.

"One of our technicians fished it out of the aquarium, and we called you," Claire said.

"Are any employees missing?" JD asked dryly.

Claire shot him a look. "I don't think so. I'm no expert, but by the looks of things, this was ingested at least several days ago."

"You have surveillance footage?" I asked.

Claire shook her head.

"I suppose no visitors have gone missing recently?" I asked.

"This particular aquarium is not accessible to visitors. The only aquariums that visitors could actually fall in are the small pools that contain the rays and other fish."

"So, only employees would have access to this area."

Claire nodded.

"I'll need a list of all employees."

"Certainly." She hesitated for a moment. "I'm concerned about the rest of the body."

"It would be helpful if we had something to connect this leg to," I said flatly.

"Well, there could be more where that came from," JD said.

Claire's face tensed with worry. "There's no need to sacrifice the shark. Our veterinarian can do an ultrasound."

It wasn't long before the medical examiner and forensics team arrived.

Dietrich snapped photos of the leg from all angles. Brenda pulled on a pair of nitrile gloves and squatted down beside the appendage, examining it carefully.

"How old do you think it is?" I asked.

"How long has the leg been severed from its owner, or are you asking how old the owner is?"

"Both would be helpful."

"It's hard to say how much the shark's digestive enzymes affected decomposition, but I'd say it's probably a week old. I can tell you the approximate age of the victim when I get the leg back to the lab."

"You said the shark's been in the tank for a week?" I asked Claire.

She nodded. "Five days, to be exact."

"You're sure about that?"

"I can look at the register, but yes, I'm sure."

"We could be looking at a couple different scenarios," I said. "Somebody either fell into the aquarium, and the rest of the remains have been devoured."

"Or somebody decided to use the shark tank as a garbage disposal and dump body parts in it," JD muttered.

Claire shivered.

"Or this shark nibbled on somebody in the open ocean before it came here," I added.

Brenda's eyes narrowed at the remains. "I think I can narrow it down for you. The shark didn't sever this leg from the owner's body."

"How can you be so sure about that?" Claire asked.

"The cut is too clean. This was done with a hacksaw or Sawzall. I can look at the tool marks when I get back to the lab."

Claire's face went pale, and she cringed. "You mean somebody dismembered a corpse and potentially tossed the remains into the aquarium?"

She looked like she was about to faint.

"That's a distinct possibility," I said.

Claire turned green and swallowed hard. Her stomach gurgled, and her cheeks bulged. She looked uneasy. "If you'll excuse me for a moment."

She hurried to the restroom.

I snapped a few photos of the appendage for reference, then talked to the engineering technician assigned to the tank, Sam Martin. He was early 40s with dark hair starting to gray around the sides. He had a narrow tan face with a large nose and walnut eyes. He was trim and wore navy work pants and a pale blue work shirt with a name patch above the chest pocket.

"Have you seen any other remains in the tank?" I asked.

Sam shook his head. "Believe me. I would have contacted you right away."

"Let us know if anything else turns up."

He nodded.

"I take it that leg doesn't look familiar."

"This is the first I've seen it."

The tattoo and the ankle bracelet made it identifiable.

I asked Sam how long he'd been working at the Aquarium.

He thought for a moment. "Oh, I'd say going on 15 years now."

"You like it here?"

"I wouldn't still be doing this if I didn't. Life's too short to do a job you hate."

"What's the environment like?"

"Thinking of applying?"

I chuckled. "Just trying to get a sense of the place. Everybody get along? Team happy?"

"It's a friendly place. Everybody that works here loves animals. Sure, there are personality conflicts like any environment, but I think we're a big, relatively happy family."

"And you're sure there's no way a visitor could have gotten into the tank?"

"Like Claire said, visitors don't have access to these areas. They just see the tanks from the other side. I suppose it's possible someone could have gotten into a restricted area, but it seems unlikely. Who knows?"

"I'm kind of anxious to find out what's left in that shark's belly," JD said.

"I'm right there with you," Sam said.

6

I called Denise and asked if there had been any new missing persons reports.

"Nothing that matches the description of the victim. Not that I have much to go on." She paused. "What do you think you're going to find in that shark's belly? Nevermind. I don't want to know."

I chuckled. "I'll keep you posted."

JD and I interviewed all of the employees on site. It took a small army to keep the Aquarium running. Maintaining saltwater tanks at the proper pH was no easy task.

All employees were required to pass a background check. Major offenses and excessive moving violations would preclude employment.

Claire rejoined us after she pulled herself together.

Brenda bagged the remains, and forensic investigators stood by as we waited for the veterinarian to get up close and personal with the 1,200-pound maneater.

Sharks filter oxygen through their gills like other fish, with the exception that they must keep moving in order to breathe. Sedating them risks death, but the veterinarian had tricks for handling situations like these.

The shark was coaxed into a pen and removed from the water with a webbed lift. Its eyes were covered with a cloth, which seemed to keep the creature docile. Hoses pumped water into the shark's mouth and through the gills, keeping the toothy critter oxygenated. The veterinarian was able to do a quick ultrasound as well as a blood draw to run the shark's metabolic panel to make sure it was in optimum health. Within a matter of minutes, the shark was back in the tank and swimming free as if nothing happened.

We eagerly awaited the results of the scan.

"From what I can tell, there's nothing else in that shark's belly that resembles a human form," the vet said. "Looks like that leg is the only piece of your victim Bethany ate."

"Bethany?"

"That's the shark's name," Claire said, seeming somewhat relieved there were no more undigested human remains in the shark's bowels.

"Well, that's good news," JD said. "But where's the rest of the body? If the owner is still alive, I'm sure they're missing that leg right about now."

Claire gave JD a scornful look. I don't think she appreciated Jack's off-color remarks.

None of the employees recognized the leg or had seen any unusual activity. At this point, we didn't have much to go on.

We wrapped up at the aquarium, and by the time we exited the building, Paris Delaney and her news crew were out front. The camera rolled, and the beautiful blonde delivered her segment into the lens, the Aquarium in the background. It wasn't long before her microphone was in my face. "Deputy Wild, can you confirm the rumors that human remains were found in the shark tank?"

Paris had an uncanny ability to discover information. I would say that she was gifted, but I'm sure she paid her source handsomely. The downside was that her source was someone in the department.

"I can confirm that the unidentified leg of a female victim was discovered. If anyone has any information, please contact the Coconut County Sheriff's Department. Thank you."

I walked out of frame as Paris asked more questions. She followed with the microphone, and the camera followed her.

"You think foul play is involved?"

"I think whoever lost her leg thinks the scenario was foul."

She scowled at me playfully, the camera lens behind her unable to see her expression.

We climbed into the Porsche and drove back to the station to fill out after-action reports.

"I told you it was bizarre," Daniels said when he poked his head into the conference room as we typed on iPads under the fluorescent lighting.

"You weren't lying."

"Find out who that leg belongs to and if she's still alive."

"I seriously doubt she's alive, but we're on it."

Daniels left, and we finished the paperwork.

"I don't know about you, but I'm starving," JD said.

"I could eat."

"I'm thinking Great White."

I groaned. "Really?"

It was a restaurant on Oyster Avenue that offered a variety of seafood dishes as well as burgers and grilled chicken sandwiches. It was adorned with pictures of maneaters, giant jawbones, and replications of sharks that hung from the ceiling. Ironically, shark was the only thing that wasn't on the menu.

"What? The food is good, and the ambiance seems fitting," JD said innocently.

Dietrich knocked on the door, then cracked it open. He was tall and skinny with dark hair and dark eyes. Quiet. Had that undertaker vibe, but that kind of went with the territory —he photographed pictures of dead bodies all day long. "I hope I'm not interrupting."

"Not at all," I said.

"I'm having an art show, and I'd love it if you guys could come."

"Really? That's fantastic. We wouldn't miss it."

A reserved smile tugged on Dietrich's lips. He had a stack of postcards in his hand and dealt two out to us.

The promotional image was surprising.

The postcard gave the date, location, and the name of the show, "Portraits in Death."

The image on the postcard was in muted colors, reminiscent of poorly exposed film from the '70s—grainy and desaturated, but artistic in its own way. Shot digitally. The woman's throat had been slit, and her dead, lifeless eyes were hazy. Speckles of blood on the floor surrounded her, and her hair was twisted and matted. The image was a head and shoulders shot, but the woman was nude. It looked like a crime scene photo, and my first inclination was that these shouldn't be the subject of an art show. I had to say I grew a little irritated but refrained from saying anything until I knew more. "This is an interesting choice of subject matter, Dietrich."

7

"Don't worry," he said. Those aren't real photos. The girl is still alive. This is a showcase of my photography and my special-effects skills. I really want to get into horror films. All the subjects are my friends and volunteered for this. The idea is to remind ourselves of our own mortality in the hopes that we can better appreciate the time that we're given."

A wave of relief washed over me. "I think that's a good message. And from what I've seen here, your special-effects work is top-notch."

Dietrich smiled again. "You guys will come to the show?"

"We'll be there," JD said.

Dietrich grinned excitedly and backed out of the conference room.

JD muttered, "That guy is a strange cat."

We headed to Oyster Avenue after we finished and had lunch at Great White. I ordered the 6-ounce filet mignon with butter-poached Maine lobster tail and bacon-wrapped sea scallops with a side of green beans and a baked potato. JD went for the Atlantic salmon topped with a lobster cream sauce, grilled sea scallops, and fried shrimp with broccoli and a side of fries.

It was reasonably priced, and the food was good. We sat at a high-top table near the bar, and I caught glimpses of the flatscreen display. It was tuned to a 24-hour news channel. Sometime during lunch, there was a breaking news report about a Hollywood actress who had mangled her car in the wee hours of the morning on the twisty Canyon Road in the Hollywood Hills. Then Scarlett's mugshot flashed on the screen.

I cringed and motioned to the TV. "You might want to take a look at this."

With a mouthful, JD craned his neck over his shoulder and looked at the display just in time to catch a glimpse of his daughter on the screen. It was followed by a clip from *Ultra Mega 2* and the lower banner read *Scarlett Nicole arrested for DUI after accident.*

JD grumbled a few obscenities as he swallowed a mouthful. His face reddened, and the veins in his neck bulged. I called my agent, Joel, right away.

He answered his cell phone on the first ring. "I'm on top of it. I'm trying to get her out now, but it takes 24 hours to process through the system. You two were my next call."

"Is she okay?" I asked.

Jack hung on the conversation. I put it on speakerphone and set the phone on the table between us.

"She was taken to the hospital and treated for minor injuries. She's fine. I've got her SPN number. She was arraigned this morning."

"When did this happen?"

"I think it was around 3 AM."

"What happened?" JD asked.

"I think she had a little too much to drink at a party and was driving too fast through the canyons."

"I'm on the next plane out," JD said.

"No need. I've got the situation taken care of."

"I appreciate that, but she's going to get a piece of my mind."

"Believe me, she's gonna get an ear full from me as well. This is the last kind of publicity she needs. Everything has been going great until now. I talked to Susan at the studio. They are upset, but they are willing to stand behind her. They have a lot of money invested in the franchise, and they want to see her succeed." Joel paused. "At least she didn't kill anybody."

"She's not even old enough to drink," JD said. "Not like that ever stopped her, but getting behind the wheel is just stupidity."

"I've already talked to a publicist. We are all in agreement with Susan that Scarlett is going into a treatment facility program before production begins on *Ultra Mega 3*, which will delay things a few weeks. As it stands, the studio might not be able to get insurance on the production. I'm gonna let her know she's really close to seeing this whole thing go away. Nobody tolerates this kind of nonsense anymore. It's not like the old days of Hollywood excess. You gotta be a major star with a box office draw to get away with these kinds of shenanigans."

JD fumed.

"We appreciate you looking after her," I said. "Let us know when you know something. In the meantime, I'll try to keep JD from short-circuiting."

Joel chuckled. "We'll talk soon."

Jack grumbled some more. "I don't know what the girl was thinking."

"She clearly wasn't."

"She's gonna piss this all away."

"I got it covered here if you want to go out there."

His face tensed, and he thought for a moment. "What's the point? I can yell at her over the phone just as well as I can in person. She may or may not listen to me either way. Besides, we've got a killer to put away. Maybe two."

8

"Got a call from a guy who thinks the leg might belong to his sister," Denise said, her soothing voice crackling through the speaker in my phone.

"What makes him think that?" I asked.

"He saw Paris Delaney's report. Recognized the ankle bracelet and tattoo. I'm not sure where she got the photo of the appendage."

"I texted her a picture of the foot and ankle. I thought it might be helpful."

"He's on his way to see Brenda. Might want to get over there. His name is Joe DiCarlo."

"Thanks for the info," I said.

"My pleasure," she sang in a cheery voice.

I ended the call, and we finished lunch. JD picked up the tab, and I told him we needed to head to the medical examiner's office.

Joe DiCarlo was 19 years old. He was a handsome kid with a square jaw, narrow brown eyes, strong brow, and chiseled features. He was about 6-feet tall and muscular.

"Yep, that's my sister's leg," he said, examining the appendage on the stainless steel table in the lab.

The stark white room was antiseptic. The cabinets were filled with chemicals and supplies. There were beakers and burners, microscopes, centrifuges, red biohazard waste containers, and boxes of nitrile gloves.

We all huddled around the remains.

"You sure about that," I said.

Joe nodded. "Between the tattoo and ankle bracelet, I'm positive."

He didn't seem too upset about it.

"When was the last time you saw her?"

He shrugged. "A few weeks ago, I guess. We didn't talk a lot."

"I take it you two weren't close."

"Not particularly. We didn't really get along. I think we kind of tolerated each other."

"Bad blood?" JD asked.

"Oh, just a little," he said in an understated tone. "She blew my fucking inheritance."

That piqued my curiosity. "How so?"

"Fawn *loved* to spend money."

"You're speaking about her in the past tense," I said.

"Well, her leg is in the medical examiner's office," Joe said dryly. "I'm assuming that she's passed on. Where's the rest of her body?"

"We don't know yet. Do you know if she ever visited the Aquarium?"

He shrugged. "I don't know. Like I said, we didn't talk a lot."

"You seem pretty mad about the inheritance."

"You're damn right I'm mad. Our parents died when I was 16. They left 3 million in a trust that was supposed to be split between the two of us. She was the trustee and somehow managed to burn through all of it before I turned 18. The bitch did it on purpose."

"That's a lot of money to burn through."

"You're telling me. She's got nothing to show for it. Parties, vacations, clothes, furniture, jewelry, cars. She went through it quick."

"You get anything out of it?"

"She bought me a car and paid my rent."

"How do you know it's all gone?"

"Because she had to start selling her ass to make ends meet."

I lifted a curious brow and exchanged a glance with JD.

"Tell me more."

"What's there to tell? She liked to call herself a yacht bunny or a professional girlfriend, but she was a hooker. Let's not mince words. She hooked up with these rich dudes for weekend getaways, or took vacations to Europe, or lounged on somebody's yacht. They gave her gifts, paid her rent, gave her cash, whatever. You can jump through all the mental hoops you want, but when somebody is compensating you for access to your private parts, that pretty much makes you a whore."

"Do you know who some of her clients were?"

"No. I tried to stay out of her life. The only thing I wanted from her was a couple grand a month to cover my rent and expenses."

"And she kept paying you?"

"For the most part. She was always trying to weasel out of it. Sometimes she'd come up short. But she owed me."

"What about friends, boyfriends?"

"Real boyfriends? You mean, like ones that didn't pay? You need to talk to Serenity Williams. That was her best friend. If anybody knows anything, it's her." He paused. "Fawn didn't really manage relationships well. May come as a shock to you, I know," he said dryly. "The closest thing she had to a real boyfriend was JC Egan. Poor bastard. He was so head over heels for her. Didn't know she was screwing half the island until they'd been dating for like six months."

"How did he take the news of her profession?" I asked.

"He flipped out. How do you think he took it? How would you take it? *Oh, by the way, honey, you don't mind if I suck a little extra dick for money, do you?*"

Brenda tried to stifle a reaction.

"You mentioned she was bad with finances. Did she owe anybody any money?"

"I don't know. Wouldn't surprise me."

"What about drugs?"

He snorted. "Kinda goes with the lifestyle. I mean, there's been mountains of cocaine on every yacht I've ever been on. But what does this have to do with anything? She got chomped by a shark?"

"Someone cut off her leg," I said.

Joe cringed. "Then fed it to a shark?"

"Judging by the tool marks, I'm pretty sure it was a Sawzall or some type of electric device," Brenda confirmed.

Joe cringed again.

"Know anybody who'd want to cut off your sister's leg?" I asked.

9

"Like I said, talk to Serenity. She's more apt to know the ins and outs of Fawn's life," Joe said.

I gave him my card and told him to contact me if he could think of anything else that might be helpful.

"What do you make of that guy?" JD asked after Joe left.

"I don't think he carved up his sister," I said. "He seemed more concerned about losing a source of revenue than losing a sibling."

"He was pretty cold about it," Brenda added.

I called Denise and filled her in. I put it on speaker. "Our victim's name is Fawn DiCarlo. See what you can find out about her."

The clack of her fingers against the keys filtered through the speaker. "Ooh, pretty girl," she said, looking at Fawn's DMV photo. "21 years old. 5'3", blonde hair, blue eyes. I'll send you a photo."

A moment later, the image buzzed my phone. Fawn was definitely a looker. Sandy blonde hair, stunning eyes, sculpted brows, pouty lips. The kind of woman that puts butterflies in your stomach. The kind you fall for, despite your better judgment. If the crappy DMV photo made you look hot, you definitely had something going on. Fawn had a focused determination in her eyes. This was a girl who knew what she wanted and knew how to get it.

Too bad she got more than she bargained for.

Denise continued. "Prior DUI. Dismissed. A few moving violations. This is interesting..."

I waited for the gorgeous redhead to continue.

"Fawn has quite the history. She was questioned in the death of Ed Trammell."

"Who's Ed Trammell?"

"Former CEO of Trammell-Tech Industries. Massive heart attack. Was found naked aboard his yacht almost a year ago with enough cocaine in his system to kill an ox. Lines of cocaine on the nightstand. Apparently, Fawn was the last person to see him alive. She was questioned at the time, but no charges were filed."

I exchanged a glance with JD.

"That girl could give me a heart attack anytime," Jack muttered. "Just saying."

Brenda rolled her eyes.

"Hard to say if it was caused by their extracurricular activities or the illicit substance," I said.

"Maybe a combination of both," Brenda added.

"Looks like Ed's wife filed a wrongful death civil suit against Fawn," Denise said. "It was also dismissed. Ed's wife's name is Ella Trammell."

"I would imagine Fawn wasn't her favorite person," I said.

"That could be a motive for murder," JD said.

"I'll need Ella's contact info," I said to Denise.

"Sure thing. But wait, there's more," she said in an infomercial voice. "Fawn was a person of interest, along with the billionaire Flynn Westwood, in the disappearance of Owen Ferguson."

"I remember something about that," I said. "Who investigated that?"

"Adams and Nelson. They worked both cases."

"Looks like we've got a few people to talk to."

I thanked Denise for the info and ended the call.

"Who do you want to talk to first?" JD asked.

10

"What's this I hear about Professor Matthews?" Paris asked when she called.

"I'm sorry, I can't hear you," I said. The wind swirled around as we cruised across the island with the top down.

"Cut the shit, Tyson."

"He's a person of interest."

"Got anything solid. Anything I can run with?"

"Not yet."

"On a scale of 1 to 10, how likely do you think it is that he's the Coed Killer?"

"9.5," I said.

"Impressive."

"It will be impressive when I nail him."

"I'll see what I can stir up," she said in a mischievous tone.

"I have no doubt." She was good at stirring things up.

"Talk to you later, Deputy Wild."

JD pulled into the parking lot of the Trident Tower. The luxury high-rise was the epitome of style and sophistication. It was home to young professionals, local celebrities, tech types, and even a few gangsters. It was attached to a marina, had a 24-hour valet and concierge, and every imaginable amenity—weight room, sauna, indoor pool.

JD pulled under the awning to the valet stand. He hopped out, flashed his badge, and told the attendant to keep it close.

At the main entrance, I waved to the concierge, and the beautiful blonde buzzed us in. She smiled from behind her desk. "Good afternoon, Deputy Wild."

"Good afternoon!"

"Who are you here to arrest today?"

I chuckled. "Nobody yet."

"The day is young," she snarked.

"It is indeed."

We made our way to the elevator bank and pressed the call button. A moment later, the door slid open, and we stepped aboard. With the press of a button we were whisked up to the 14th floor. A quick stroll down the hallway put us in front of #1402.

JD knocked.

A woman's muffled voice filtered through the door. "Who is it?"

I held my badge up to the peephole. "Deputy Wild. We spoke on the phone a few moments ago."

A gorgeous platinum blonde pulled open the door wearing an almost sheer white halter dress that revealed plenty of cleavage and side boob. Serenity had striking features, a perfect smile, and a delightful, petite figure.

Fawn had classic features and a sophisticated allure, whereas Serenity was the type of bottle-blonde you'd see on the cover of Hot Rod magazines or the main stage at *Forbidden Fruit*. Drool-worthy in a more over-the-top kind of way, whereas Fawn had a subtle, smoldering quality.

"What's this about? You were kind of vague on the phone. I'm not in any kind of trouble, am I?"

"No, ma'am. We need to ask you a few questions about Fawn."

"What has she done now?"

I filled her in on the situation.

Her eyes rounded, and her jaw dropped. Tears welled, then streamed down her cheeks. "Are you sure it's her?"

"Her brother made a positive identification, but we still can't say with certainty whether she's alive or dead."

She wiped her eyes and stepped aside. "Please, come in."

We entered the condo, and she led us down the foyer to the living room. It was a nice unit. There were floor-to-ceiling windows in the living room and sliding glass doors that opened to a large terrace. The floors were bleached hardwoods, and Serenity had decorated the place with white leather furniture, glass coffee and end tables, and colorful abstract art on the walls. The kind of paintings you could get at a Swedish furniture store—mass-market stuff. There was a flatscreen display, a stereo, plants in the corners, and a prissy white cat that reminded me of Fluffy. The kitchen had marble countertops and new stainless steel appliances. There was a single bedroom just off the living room.

"I can't believe this happened," Serenity said.

"When was the last time you spoke with Fawn?" I asked.

"I've been out of town for the last two weeks. It was sometime before that, I guess."

"You two were close, right?"

She nodded. "She was my best friend." Her eyes teared up again. "I mean, you're not *saying* she's dead, but she's dead, right? That's a pretty major body part to lose and not turn up in a hospital somewhere."

I gave a grim nod.

A few more tears trickled down her smooth skin. She grabbed a Kleenex from the coffee table and blotted her eyes, her mascara starting to run.

"You were saying you were out of town."

She nodded. "I was in Greece. Mykonos. Have you been?"

I nodded. "Beautiful place."

"Did you go alone? With a friend?"

Her eyes narrowed ever so slightly. "An acquaintance."

It was a measured answer.

"Are you in the same line of work as Fawn?"

11

"And what line of work would that be?" Serenity asked cautiously.

After a momentary pause, I said, "Companionship."

She hesitated.

"Don't worry. I'm not interested in your career path. I just need to get to the truth."

The tension left her face. She exhaled a breath. "I'm a very good companion."

"I have no doubt."

"Can you think of any of Fawn's clients who may have wished to harm her?"

She shook her head. "Everybody loved Fawn. Have you seen her? The girl was stunning. Everyone wanted her." She pulled up a picture of Fawn on her phone and showed it to me. A rather provocative picture.

Stunning was an understatement.

"What do you know about Ed Trammell?"

She shrugged uncomfortably. "What does that have to do with this?"

"Maybe nothing. Maybe a motive for revenge."

"You think his wife could've had her killed?" Serenity asked.

"I think anything is a possibility at this point."

Her face tensed. "That bitch."

"Tell me how you really feel," JD snarked.

"Hey, the guy wanted company. His wife clearly wasn't doing it for him. Fawn took care of his need."

"His need for an excessive amount of cocaine?" I asked.

"His need for intimacy. All I know is that Fawn told me that he was alive when she left."

"Do you believe her?"

"I told you, she was my best friend. She had no reason to lie to me."

"How did Ed Trammell get the drugs?" I asked.

"How does anybody get drugs?"

"Maybe Fawn supplied them?"

"Or maybe he had them before?" Her face tensed again. "Look, are you trying to make her look bad, or are you trying to find out what happened to her?"

"I'm just trying to collect as much information as I can. I'm primarily concerned with who may have wanted to cut her up and feed her to a shark."

Serenity cringed and shivered. "That's horrible."

"What about Flynn Westwood?"

She took a deep breath and tried not to look irritated. "I introduced them."

"Really? You always share clients?"

"He said he wanted two girls. I brought Fawn along. I guess he liked her better."

"You lost him as a client?"

"Well, he kept calling Fawn after that. He didn't call me."

"How did that make you feel?"

Her eyes narrowed at me. "It made me feel kind of shitty. How do you think it made me feel? But when you're friends with someone like Fawn, you get used to playing second fiddle."

"Do I detect a hint of jealousy?" JD asked.

She gave him a look. "Look, guys have different preferences. That's all. Some guys preferred Fawn. I tried not to take it personally."

"Seems like that could be hard to do."

"It's business. It's not like I'm emotionally attached to any of my clients."

"But that's got to suck when they ditch you for your best friend."

"Sometimes life sucks, sometimes it doesn't."

"What do you know about Owen Ferguson's disappearance?" I asked.

She hesitated again. "I know that they all went out one afternoon, and he didn't come back. He probably got drunk and fell overboard."

"Did you know him personally?"

"I partied with Flynn and Owen once."

"What was their relationship like?"

"I think they were good friends. Why don't you ask Flynn?"

"I plan on it."

We stared at each other for a moment.

"What about her ex-boyfriend, JC Egan?"

Serenity sighed, and her face saddened. "Poor guy. He's really cute and sweet. He just got in over his head. I mean, Fawn was always out of his league. And he was so naïve. I mean, I told Fawn she needed to be upfront with him, but she always wanted to have her cake and eat it too."

"Did he ever express any anger when things went south?"

"He was devastated. And there were a few harsh words." She thought about it for a moment. "Maybe more than a few. It got kinda heated."

"What kind of harsh words?"

"Whore, slut, bitch, tramp... you know, terms of endearment." Serenity smirked. "I mean, you can call me those names in the bedroom. I kinda like it. But you better not call me a bitch in an argument."

"Was he ever violent?"

"No. Never. But, I guess he did make some threatening comments on social media."

"Such as?"

"He said he hoped she ended up in a wood chipper." Serenity's face crinkled. "That's kinda creepy, isn't it?"

"It's concerning," I said understatedly. "Tell me about some of her other clients."

12

"She didn't want to overwork herself," Serenity said. "At this level, she didn't need too many clients. Just a few infatuated regulars to cover her monthly expenses and then some."

"And who were some of these *infatuated clients*?" I asked.

"Besides Flynn, there was Roman Ellington and Simon Brennan."

"What can you tell me about them?"

"Roman's sweet. Older. 50s. Still good-looking, though. He's retired. Sold his company. He's got a little money, but not Flynn Westwood money."

"What about Simon Brennan?"

She shrugged. "He's okay. He's like a jewelry guy."

"Diamond dealer," JD said. "He's got a shop in town."

"You know where I can find these gentlemen?"

She nodded.

"Roman lives in the Fillmore. Simon's got a yacht at Sandpiper Point."

"Do you have contact information for them?"

She nodded again.

"Text it to me."

She took a deep, uncomfortable breath. "I don't usually give out client information," she said, searching for words. "Discretion is part of the job. It would ruin my reputation if you said I spoke to you about them."

"I have resources. I can find their information. This just makes it easier. And I won't say anything."

"Promise?"

"I promise."

The fluffy white cat rubbed up against my shins affectionately.

Serenity shifted onto one hip, and her lips crinkled as she stared into my eyes, trying to determine if she could trust me. "Well, Princess seems to like you. So I guess you're okay."

She looked up the contact information for the two gentlemen and JC Egan and texted the numbers to me.

I gave her my card as she walked us to the door.

"If there's anything else—"

"I'll be sure to call you." She pulled open the door. "I hope you find out what happened to her. I mean, you can't blow this off because she was a... you know."

"Trust me, we're not gonna blow this off."

We left the condo and ambled down the hallway to the elevator. Serenity closed her apartment door behind us.

"How much do you think she charges?" JD asked.

I arched an eyebrow at him.

"Just curious," he said innocently.

We reached the elevators, and JD pressed the call button.

My phone buzzed with a call from Isabella.

"The last GPS data I have for Fawn DiCarlo's phone is at the *Aegaeon*. Before that, it was at the Fillmore Tower in the early evening last Thursday."

"What a coincidence. Roman Ellington happens to live in the Fillmore Tower."

"Should that name mean something to me?" Isabella asked.

"Just a client of Fawn's. How long was the phone there?"

"Not long. Maybe 15 minutes. Then it made its way back to the Aegaeon, where it remained till the next day. Then went off the grid. I'm assuming the battery died."

"Can you pinpoint the exact last location of the phone?"

"The parking garage, according to the elevation data."

I thanked Isabella and ended the call.

"Something happened in that parking lot," JD said.

"Let's see if there's any surveillance footage."

"I want to know how she went from a parking lot to the belly of a shark."

"I guess that is what we're going to find out."

We stepped onto the elevator and headed down to the lobby. I said goodbye to the concierge, and we pushed through the main doors. The valet hustled to bring JD's Porsche 15 feet. Jack gave the gentleman a nice tip, and we hopped in and drove across town to the Aegaeon.

It was a five-story luxury apartment building with parking underneath and a secure lobby. It was a nice place, but certainly not the Trident Tower. It lacked the amenities and personal services. I'm not exactly sure what type of money Fawn was bringing in from her companion services or what kind of debt she was carrying, but I assumed she wanted to keep her expenses low, considering she was also assisting her brother. Not that the Aegaeon was cheap, just that it wasn't quite as expensive as the Trident.

We pulled into the visitor parking lot, and JD found an empty space. He killed the engine, and we hopped out of the car and headed toward the lobby. The resident parking garage was gated, though it didn't take much to bypass the security system.

I dialed the property manager from the call box, and she buzzed us in. We passed through the lobby to the parking area. There were plenty of high-end cars—BMWs, Porches, Audi's, Mercedes. No Ferraris or Lamborghinis.

I searched for Fawn's cell phone but didn't find it.

"You think maybe somebody was waiting for her in the parking lot?" JD suggested. "She came home. They abducted her, took her somewhere else to carve her up and turn her into fish food."

"Something like that. Or maybe she never made it back to the apartment at all. Maybe somebody brought her phone back here to throw us off."

We made our way up to the second floor to the property manager's office. I flashed my badge and made introductions. "I noticed a security camera in the parking garage? Is it functional?"

"It was until last week when vandals spray-painted over the lens," Carol said.

"Do you know what day that was?"

"I think it was Thursday. You got a lead on the little bastards that did it?"

"No. But there may be a connection to the case we're working on. Did you notify the Sheriff's Department?"

"I called, but you're the first guys to show up. That's what I thought you were here about."

"Was there any other vandalism on the property?"

"Surprisingly, no. None of the cars were broken into. Usually, when that happens, it's thieves taking out the cameras before they do something shitty."

"A resident may have been abducted at that time."

The property manager's eyes rounded.

"Do you recall when the cameras were vandalized?"

"I think it was around 8 or 8:30PM. I can check the time-stamp on the video."

"I'd like a copy of it if you can get it to me."

"Sure. Who went missing?"

"Fawn DiCarlo."

Carol lifted her brow, and her eyes widened. "Really? That's terrible. Such a pretty young girl." She shrugged. "But you know, I think she liked to live in the fast lane. Not saying she brought it on herself. But you gotta keep your wits about you."

Her pudgy fingers punched the keyboard, and she pulled up the surveillance footage. She scrolled through the timeline, then spun the monitor around to face us and pressed play. It was difficult to see—the footage was dark and grainy.

13

There was only one camera angle in the parking garage. A figure clad in black wearing a ski mask blurred into the garage after a vehicle exited. He slipped into the shadows and managed to stay out of the camera's view until a spray can popped up and blacked out the optics. There was no way to identify the perpetrator.

"I'm not very technically savvy, but if you can find a way to export the clip, you can have it," Carol said.

She offered me her chair, and I slid behind her desk, spun the monitor back around, and fumbled with the application. After a few minutes of messing around with it, I figured out how to do it and emailed the clip to myself.

I stood up and gave her the chair back.

"When was the last time you saw Fawn?"

Her face crinkled as she thought. "I don't recall."

"She ever have any trouble here?"

"I don't think I ever got any complaints about her or from her. I don't think she was here a lot, honestly. She had a lot of *friends* if you know what I mean? Male friends. I think she was always off gallivanting around somewhere. But hey, what do I know?"

"I'm sure you hear things," I said.

A sly grin tugged her lips. "These walls talk. They're paper-thin. And some tenants love to gossip."

I gave her my card. "We may have more questions."

"Call me anytime, Deputy," Carol said with a smile that was almost flirty.

We left the office and took the elevator down to the lobby, and pushed into the visitor parking lot. I was in a hurry to speak with Roman Ellington.

We headed over to the Fillmore. It was a lot like the Trident, just older. It had a concierge and valet, but it didn't have quite the same amenities. There was an attached marina filled with yachts, sailboats, and speedboats. The demographic was a little older. The building was quieter on Friday and Saturday nights.

We pulled up to the valet and went through the usual routine. A flash of my badge got us into the lobby, and we made our way up to the 26th floor and banged on the door to Roman's condo.

There was no answer.

I banged again, and still no response.

After waiting a few minutes, we headed back down to the lobby, and I spoke with the concierge. He was a slender guy in his mid 20s with brown hair, brown eyes, and a well-manicured face. I asked him if he had seen Roman.

"I'm sorry, I haven't. Our residents value their privacy, and I try not to make note of their comings and goings." He flashed an insincere smile, and I got the distinct impression that he wasn't a fan of law enforcement.

I gave him an unappreciative stare, and I think that made him a little uncomfortable.

"He does have a yacht in the marina," he said, unsettled. "Perhaps you might want to look there, Deputy." He was trying to be helpful, but it still came off as smug.

"The name?"

His face crinkled as he thought. "I'm not really sure. *Silicon Dreams*. That's it."

"Thank you. I would appreciate it if you keep our visit confidential."

"Like I said, I stay out of the business of the residents."

We pushed outside and ambled down to the dock, looking for the boat. It was a 67-foot *SunTrekker* with a Navy hull and white trim. It was a nice boat. Roman had done more than okay for himself. *Silicon Dreams* was painted across the transom in an old-school computer font.

We crossed the gangway, stepped to the aft deck, and banged on the sliding glass door to the salon. We waited a few minutes, but there was no response. We hung out for a few minutes, then decided to leave.

The valet pulled the car around. We hopped in and pulled away. We would have to catch up with Roman later.

I called Denise and had her pull the registration records for Simon Brennan as we headed across the island to Sand-piper Point. The upscale marina was home to superyachts and bluewater sailboats. It catered to high-end clientele—lots of former Silicon Valley tech types that had relocated.

"Mr. Sparkles," Denise said.

"That's the name of his boat?"

"Yep."

I had to chuckle.

We were at the marina in a matter of minutes. The parking lot was filled with exotic sports cars and luxury SUVs. We made our way to the dock and searched for *Mr. Sparkles*.

14

Mr. Sparkles was a 147' *Bassani Vento Veloce*. It had sleek, windswept lines and elegant curves. There was an alfresco dining area on the aft deck, and a sliding glass door led to an opulent salon. There was a bridge deck and a sky deck above that. We crossed the transom and banged on the sliding glass door. I had no doubt we were visible on the security cameras.

A moment later, a burly dude marched through the salon. He was thick and stocky, with a dark beard, narrow eyes, and hair trimmed short on the sides, with a little length on top. He had a hard, focused look about him.

I flashed my badge when he pulled open the door. "What can I do for you?"

"Need to speak with Simon Brennan."

"What's this in regard to?"

"The disappearance of Fawn DiCarlo."

"Wait here."

He disappeared into the salon and down the forward passageway.

Simon Brennan returned a moment later. He was a handsome man in his mid 40s with a trimmed beard and longish hair combed back over his ears. His piercing blue eyes and square jaw made him a hit with the ladies, and he had just the right amount of wrinkles around the eyes to make him look dignified.

He had a swarthy tan and wore a pale-blue short-sleeve Oxford button-down shirt and white pants with deck shoes. The Rolex Oyster Perpetual Milgauss on his wrist was understated elegance for a man of his wealth—sleek silver with an aqua face. Nobody needed a $14,000 watch to tell time. It was a fashion accessory.

He flashed a charming smile that I'm sure had melted a few panties in its time. "Good afternoon, gentlemen. Archer tells me you're here about Fawn DiCarlo. I saw the news report. It's terrible. Is there anything I can do to help?"

Traces of his cologne wafted in the air. *Voltolini Pour Homme* —$9,000 a bottle.

"You can tell me the last time you saw her," I said.

"Certainly." He paused and thought. "It's been a few weeks. Do you know when she went missing?"

"We suspect last Thursday."

"From the news report, I take it she is deceased?"

"One would assume, but we haven't made a determination yet."

"But it's technically a homicide investigation, right?"

"Not yet."

He took a breath. "Like I said, it was probably two weeks ago. I can check my schedule and get back with you."

"I would appreciate that. What did you do when you last saw her?"

He stared at me for a moment with a sly grin, contemplating how to answer. "She came over. We had dinner, drinks, and I enjoyed her company."

"I take it you were having a sexual relationship with her?"

"I don't like to kiss and tell, Deputy, but that's pretty safe to assume."

"Was it strictly a business transaction, or was there an emotional connection?"

"I really liked Fawn. She was an ambitious girl. She had her qualities, and she was good company. But I don't let myself get attached to unavailable women."

"You don't seem like the type of guy who needs to pay for it," I said.

He smirked. "We all pay for it, don't we, Deputy?"

JD kept his mouth shut.

"I find it's easier," Simon said. "Less complicated. We both know the score, and everybody leaves happy. No messy entanglements. No sticky situations. No unwarranted allegations. All of the women sign written contracts acknowledging their role and responsibility, and what actions will and won't take place. You know how it is these days—one false allegation can ruin a man's reputation and destroy his wealth. Someone in my position needs to be exceedingly cautious."

"Looks like you've done well for yourself in the diamond industry."

"I have, but there is always room to grow."

"How frequently did you see Fawn?"

"Perhaps once a week over the last several months."

"That seems quite often."

"We had an arrangement."

"You must have liked her quite a bit to see her that often."

"I liked what we had. I enjoyed our time together. She was a talented girl."

"Yet you developed no feelings for her," I said.

His eyes narrowed at me. "Are you suggesting I'm cold and calloused, Deputy?"

"I'm just curious how you spend that much time with someone and not develop any emotional bonds."

He shrugged. "Maybe you should speak with my therapist," he joked. "I have an ability to compartmentalize. I've found it helps me look at business relationships objectively. I don't get emotional about business decisions, stocks, or women. All three can make you wealthy, and they can also destroy you."

JD stifled a comment. With six ex-wives, he knew a thing or two about being on the wrong end of a bad relationship.

"I don't see how my feelings about Fawn are relevant to the situation," Simon said.

"Just trying to understand the nature of your relationship. That's all."

"Am I a person of interest?"

"We are speaking with everyone who had interaction with Fawn. I'm sure you understand."

"Of course. And I'm happy to assist. Just because I didn't love her doesn't mean I don't care about her well-being. There is a distinction."

"Can you tell me where you were last Thursday evening?"

"If I recall correctly, I was here on the boat, enjoying a cocktail and a nice dinner."

"Alone?"

"Apart from my security staff. You met Archer Lynch. His brother Cole is around here somewhere if you would like to speak with them."

"Do you have protection 24 hours a day, seven days a week?" I asked.

"I quite often handle a lot of cash and valuable jewelry. I recognize that I am a high-profile target. I think it would be foolish to go without protection."

I asked him a few more questions, then spoke with Archer and Cole. They looked nearly identical, apart from a few obvious differences. They had the same eyes and square jaw. Cole's beard was a little longer and bushier, but he didn't have any hair on top. His head was cue-ball slick. His nose was wider and looked like he had taken a few more punches. They both were rough-and-tumble bruisers that could handle themselves in a bar fight or on a battlefield.

I thanked them for their cooperation, and we left *Mr. Sparkles* behind. I called Isabella as we ambled down the dock to the parking lot. "What can you tell me about Archer and Cole Lynch?"

15

Isabella's fingers clacked against the keyboard. "Archer Lynch. Former military. Airborne Rangers. Same with Cole. They're a little over a year apart. Archer is older. A few assault charges here and there. Brawling mostly. Other than that, they're clean. A few moving violations and parking tickets. Nothing outstanding."

"Thanks," I said. "What about Simon Brennan?"

Her fingers danced again. "Owns Key Diamond International. Again, not much. A few moving violations. A possession charge from the '90s. If he's dirty, I don't see it."

While I had her on the phone, I asked her to track Roman's cell.

"Looks like he's at the Country Club right now," Isabella said. "If you hustle, you might catch him as he's coming off the 18th."

"We're on it."

I ended the call, and we jogged through the parking lot to the Porsche. JD zipped across the island to the posh country club. We'd been given an honorary membership due to our efforts in a previous case. The security guard waved us in, and we pulled into the parking lot. JD parked the car not far from the 18th green, and we jogged over and waited on the cart path near one of the sand traps. The smell of fresh-cut grass lingered in the air.

I had Denise send me Roman's DMV photo, and I scanned the foursomes as they reached the green. We watched a couple groups play out the hole. Some were good, some were not so good. They sunk their putts and congratulated one another, giving us curious looks as they shuffled off the green and back onto their carts.

A ball crackled through the trees and plowed into the sand trap a few yards away from us.

Another ball hit the back of the green and spun back toward the cup. It stopped about 4 feet away. We waited for the two members to arrive. They pulled to the green in an electric cart, hopped out, and grabbed their clubs. One brought a sand wedge to the trap, while the other took his putter to the green. Roman was the one sitting 4 feet from the pin.

The guy in the sand trap gave us a curious glance and said, "Maybe I should charge you guys to watch."

He had a cocky grin on his face as he lined up the shot. He drew the clubhead back and smacked the sand with a thump. The thick white sand flew through the air, launching the ball to the edge of the sand trap. It hit the lip and rolled back down the berm.

The guy grumbled a few obscenities.

"You must be on the pro tour," JD teased.

The man shot him a look, his face turning red. He dug his feet in the sand, steadied himself, and drew the clubhead back.

Whack!

More sand.

The ball flopped through the air, hit the lip, and rolled back down the berm, past its original position, back to the far side of the sand trap.

"Maybe crowds make you nervous," JD said.

By this time, the guy's face was beet red. He glared at Jack, then lined up again and took a shot.

This time, he managed to clear the edge of the sand trap. The ball flew over the green and into the other one, leaving a trail of white sand speckled across the green.

The man glared at us, mumbled a few obscenities, then stomped across the green to the other sand trap.

Roman had marked his ball and waited patiently at the edge of the green. He kept giving us curious glances.

Finally, Mr. Sandtrap got on the green but was still farther away from the pin than Roman.

It took him three putts before we all heard that satisfying clunk of a Titleist dropping into the cup.

Roman knocked his ball in with one smooth stroke. He bent over and plucked the balls from the hole and tossed one back to Mr. Sandtrap, then replaced the pin. The two men walked down the slope of the green, Mr. Sandtrap glaring at us.

JD flashed his badge as we approached. "Roman Ellington?"

His brow knitted together, and his eyes narrowed. "That's me."

"We'd like to talk to you about Fawn DiCarlo."

His face tightened. "What about her?"

"I take it you haven't been watching the news today," I said.

"No, I haven't."

"Fawn is... missing."

"What!?"

I filled him in on the situation, and his face went pale, his throat tightened, and his eyes misted. He said to Mr. Sandtrap, "I'll catch up with you at the clubhouse."

Mr. Sandtrap gave him a nod, gave us a dirty glance, then took the clubs and marched back to the cart. He stuffed both of them in the bags, then climbed behind the wheel and stepped on the pedal. The electric motor whined, and the tires barked as the golf cart lurched forward down the path.

We stepped away from the green as another ball hit the center, not far from the pin. Dead solid perfect.

I knew the answer, but I wanted to see how he'd respond. "When was the last time you saw Fawn?"

16

R oman thought for a moment. "I'm not sure. I think it was last Thursday evening."

"Where at?" I asked.

"My condo." Confusion crinkled his face. "When you say missing, you mean dead, right?"

"We don't have a full body."

A grave look washed over his face.

"Tell me what happened at your condo."

Roman was dazed. He fumbled for words. "There's not much to tell, really. She came over, stayed briefly, then left."

"Just a quickie?" JD asked.

Romans face twisted. "No. What are you talking about?"

"We are aware of the services that Fawn provided," I said.

He seemed flustered. "It wasn't like that."

"What was it like?"

"It's complicated. I don't think you'd understand."

"Trust me, I think I understand," I said. "Right now, you might be the last person to have seen Fawn DiCarlo alive."

"You think I had something to do with her disappearance?"

"Did you?"

"No," he said, his brow knitted together. "I cared deeply for Fawn." He paused, collecting his thoughts. "She deserved better. She didn't need to be doing what she was doing."

"And you were going to take care of her?" I asked.

"Yes. I wanted her to leave the lifestyle behind." His eyes flicked between the two of us. "I know, you think I'm an idiot. I fell in love with a hooker. I don't care. She's so much more than that," he said, his voice breaking up.

"So why the short visit Thursday night?" I asked

Roman took a deep breath. "I requested her company for the evening. I expressed my feelings for her, and... Let's just say she didn't feel the same way." His eyes misted. "She thought it best if we ended our professional relationship since I was getting too close. I begged her not to cut me off. She's an addiction, you know? And when it comes to her, I'm like a drug addict."

"So, she left—alive and with both legs?"

He nodded.

"I take it you weren't too happy about getting turned down," I said.

"I was devastated. How do you think I felt?"

"Angry?"

"Goddamn right I was. I thought..." He paused, choking up. His eyes welled. He took a deep breath and composed himself. "I thought we had something. I thought she felt the same way. It was different between us. Turns out she was a good actress."

"You were emotionally invested in her."

He nodded.

"Did you get violent?"

He looked at me, and his face went long. He swallowed hard. "No. I would never—"

I cut him off. "You sure about that?"

He paused again, his jaw tightened. A frustrated breath exhaled through his nose. "Okay. I lost my temper for a minute. I smacked her, and that's when she left. I apologized right away. I tried to get her to stay. I didn't mean to do it. I was just so overcome with..."

"Emotion?"

"Yeah, something like that."

"After she left your condo, she went back to her apartment," I said.

"How do you know that?"

"Her cell records."

His eyes were fixed on me.

"You sure you didn't follow her back to the parking lot of her apartment complex, confront her in the garage, and abduct her?"

His face crinkled again. "What!? No!"

"You loved her. And you couldn't bear the thought of her with somebody else. You know, *you can't have her, nobody else can*, right?"

With a tight face, he said, "No. I would never hurt Fawn. I didn't follow her back to her apartment. I didn't abduct her in the parking garage. I didn't cut off her leg and feed her to a shark!"

I exchanged a glance with JD.

"Did you try to contact her after that?"

"Of course. I sent text messages and left voicemails, but she never replied. I figured I had really blown it and that she just needed time to cool off. I mean, eventually, she had to see that we were right for each other. Nobody else was going to take care of her like I would. Nobody else would love her like I would."

Another foursome played through on the green while we had our conversation on the cart path.

"If there's a chance that she is still alive, you need to find her."

"We're doing everything we can."

"What you are doing is wasting time accusing me of something I didn't do."

"Can you think of anybody who might have wanted to see her in the belly of a shark?" I asked.

17

Roman paused as the foursome exited the green, giving us all curious stares. They got on their carts and drove away.

"No. I didn't know any of her other clients, and I didn't want to know."

"Own any power tools? A Sawzall, perhaps?"

He looked at me with mortified eyes. "A Sawzall? Is that what was used?"

"We believe so."

His stomach turned, and he looked like he was going to be sick. He hunched over and swallowed hard, trying to keep the contents of his stomach down. He turned green and tried to steady himself. "I need to sit down," he said thinly. He took a step, then collapsed. Roman fell to the grass, and JD and I attended to him.

"I'm okay. I just had a moment there."

He sat on the ground breathing deeply, sweat misting on his brow.

I thought he might have been having a heart attack. I dialed 911 and requested an ambulance.

"I'm fine," Roman assured. "That's not necessary."

The last thing the county needed was this guy to keel over after being questioned by two deputies.

"Let's just get you checked out to be sure."

An ambulance arrived a few minutes later and attended to Roman. The scene drew a curious crowd.

The EMTs did an EKG, and everything checked out. His vitals were good, though his heart rate was a little elevated along with his blood pressure. They gave him the option of going to Coconut General to get checked out, which he declined.

I figured we had questioned the guy enough for one day. I gave him my card and told him to contact us if he thought of anything that might be helpful.

Roman made his way back to the clubhouse amid the crowd of onlookers. The EMTs and paramedics packed up and went on their way, and we headed back to the parking lot.

"I don't think that guy's got it in him to saw body parts," JD said. "I think he genuinely cared for the girl."

"I think you might be right. That, or he's petrified of getting caught, and he knows we're close."

My phone buzzed with a call from Juliana Morgan. She was a professor of Occult Studies at the university. She had assisted on our previous case, though she found JD's frat party antics to be less than impressive. "What's this I hear about you harassing Professor Matthews?"

"We didn't harass him," I said. "We just asked him a few pertinent questions."

"I don't know where you're going with this, but I can assure you Professor Matthews is a well-respected educator."

"He may be a well-respected educator. But he also might be the Coed Killer."

"Before you ruin this man's life, do you have any evidence to back this up?"

"I have my own eyes."

"You saw Professor Matthews attack someone?" she asked, incredulous.

"I chased a man across campus with his exact stride. It was him. I'm sure of it."

She scoffed. "You chased a *masked* man across campus. Surely someone in your position requires a little more certainty when evaluating persons of interest."

"I'm certain."

"I'm telling you, he's not your guy."

"Then he's got nothing to worry about."

"I beg to disagree. As it stands, he's got that bitch reporter and several news crews at his doorstep, asking questions. They're ready to convict the guy in the court of public opinion without a shred of evidence."

"Like I said, we just asked him a few questions."

"I gave you guys the benefit of the doubt on the last case. And to your credit, you guys brought a killer to justice. I'm not quite sure how given your unorthodox methods. But this is absolutely unacceptable. Evan Matthews is a dear friend and a valued colleague. And I think you need to go on record and make a public statement that Professor Matthews had no involvement in the attacks on campus."

Juliana had been gracious enough not to file a formal complaint against JD after his campus shenanigans. But her current tone made it sound like she was considering holding that over our heads.

"That kinda sounds like a threat," I said lightly.

"It's not a threat, Deputy," she said in a dry, annoyed voice. "It's just the right thing to do."

She ended the call before I had a chance to respond.

I didn't have to fill JD in on the conversation. He could hear her angry voice crackling through the speaker in my phone just fine.

"You really set her off," Jack said.

"Me?" I lifted an incredulous brow. "You're the one who annoyed her first. She was ready to file a complaint about you until I smoothed things out."

JD's face crinkled dismissively. "That woman loves me. She just doesn't know it yet."

I rolled my eyes.

Juliana Morgan was gorgeous. She had anything but love for the two of us.

We hopped into the Porsche and left the country club behind. I called Denise, and she gave me JC Egan's address and place of employment. I figured talking to Fawn's ex-boyfriend was probably a good idea, especially after the wood-chipper comment.

We caught up with him at his *work*. That was an overstatement. He had a cush gig for a 22-year-old.

18

Music spilled out of the club, pumping through massive speakers. I flashed my badge to the cashier, and she waved us in. She grabbed her phone and sent a text message, presumably to the manager, to let him know deputies were on the premises.

The *Pussycat Palace* was a second-rate strip club just out of town. It wasn't a place we frequented often. It lacked the style and sophistication of *Forbidden Fruit*. It was dirtier, the drinks a little cheaper, and the entertainment a little less than high class.

The air smelled like beer, whiskey, and cheap perfume. Glycol fog flooded the stage, and spotlights slashed the air. Scantily clad girls slinked around chrome poles, undulating in provocative ways. There was a little something for everyone here. Big girls, small girls, busty girls, flat girls. Blondes, brunettes, red-heads, and alternative types with neon hair in a spectrum of colors.

We had barely taken a step into the club when we were greeted by the manager, Bert. He was an older gentleman wearing a tank top and cargo shorts. He had weathered skin and a purple Mohawk. Two small silver hoop earrings dangled from his ears, and he had a barbell through his left eyebrow. If I had to guess, I'd put Bert at about 62. A gold chain dangled around his neck, and a demeanor that was both gruff and jovial at the same time.

"What can I do for you, gentlemen?"

I flashed my badge. "I need to talk to one of your employees, JC Egan."

He pointed to the DJ booth. "He ain't in any trouble, is he?"

"Just routine," I said.

Bert forced a smile. "Hope you boys enjoy yourselves. Drinks are on the house."

Bert didn't want any trouble with the law. I figured he had plenty of people leaning on him. Everyone from the fire marshal to the mafia. He had to grease a lot of palms to run one of these businesses and not run afoul of someone.

The song ended, and the performer on the main stage gathered up her lacy bra and the dollar bills that were on the stage. She added them to the wad of greenbacks in her G-string, then sauntered down the runway to the dressing room.

JC Egan's voice boomed over the loudspeakers. "Please welcome to the stage for your viewing pleasure, Houston!" The kid had a smooth DJ voice. "Houston, we have no problems here."

Houston was a bottle blonde with an hourglass figure enhanced by lots of silicone in the lips, chest, and rear. She pranced across the stage with clear stilettos and flung a tan leg around a chrome pole.

Men drooled and threw dollar bills on stage as she taunted them with her wares, peeling off her bra as slowly as possible. When she finally tossed the frilly thing aside, she covered her headlights with her hands and taunted the audience again, eventually revealing them one by one. You could put an eye out with one of those things.

We made our way to the DJ booth. I flashed my badge and shouted over the noise. "I need to talk to you about Fawn DiCarlo."

"What do you want to know?"

"When was the last time you saw her?"

It wasn't the ideal place to conduct an interview.

JD patted me on the shoulder and moved toward the stage. We could barely hear what JC was saying anyway. Jack had his money clip out and was slipping dollar bills in Houston's appreciative G-string in no time. She squatted down beside the stage and pulled the string away from her shimmering body, giving JD enough room to slip in a bill and maybe catch a glimpse of her landing strip.

JC shook his head. "I can't talk about this right now. It's way too fresh."

"Pretty emotional, huh?"

"I loved her, man."

"That's why you commented you wished she would end up in a wood chipper?"

His face tensed. "I didn't mean it."

"Well, it wasn't a wood chipper, but somebody cut her up."

His face tensed. "I told you, I don't want to talk about this."

"If you don't talk to me, it'll make me think you had something to do with it."

He glared at me. "I'm trying to work."

"I see that. Real tough job. You've got time in between songs."

"I don't have to talk to you. You can't make me."

"I guess you really don't care all that much about Fawn, or you'd help us find out what happened."

He ignored me and leaned into the microphone when the song was wrapping up. "Give a big round of applause for Houston!"

The small crowd clapped and cheered. They hooted and hollered. JD returned to the DJ stand with a grin on his face.

I dug into my pocket and handed JC a card, just in case he had a change of heart. I left it on the ledge of the DJ stand.

JC continued to ignore me.

I asked JD if he had fun.

"You know, this place isn't my first choice. But there is talent here, and drinks are on the house. I think it would be rude if we didn't stay for at least one drink."

19

The drinks may have been on the house, but the dancers weren't. We left the club several drinks later, and a few hundred dollars lighter, smelling like cheap perfume and whiskey, all wound up with nothing to show for it.

The neon signage flickered, bathing the parking lot in pink and blue. Provocative neon shapes changed poses every few seconds.

JD clicked the alarm on the Porsche, and the lights flashed. We hopped in, and JD cranked up the engine. "Where to?"

We had skipped dinner, and my stomach was growling. "I don't know about you, but I'm hungry."

"You read my mind."

"What are you in the mood for?"

"A little blonde about 5'2"," JD said.

"Besides that."

He thought for a moment. "Pizza."

We both said in unison. "Big Tony's."

He put the car into gear and pulled out of the parking lot. We zipped back into town. The moon hung low in the sky, and the stars flickered above. The cool night air swirled about the vehicle.

If you wanted the best New York-style pizza on the island, *Big Tony's* was the place. It didn't hurt that we knew the owner and always got free pizza. Big Tony was an old-school reformed mafia guy. He was one of those guys that was instantly likable, but you knew in the old days he could be fearsome. I'm sure he smiled while busting out a few kneecaps with a baseball bat.

As soon as we walked into the joint, I noticed Juliana Morgan in a booth against the far wall. Her choice of companion for the evening was a little surprising.

The luscious redhead was a sight to behold. She had emerald eyes, porcelain skin, and an elegant way about her. She was mysterious and enigmatic and certainly captivating. What she was doing with that douche-canoe across the table from her was beyond me. I didn't think she was romantically involved with Professor Matthews. At least, I hoped not. Surely the colleagues weren't discussing academics. I couldn't see too much overlap in molecular biology and occult studies.

We placed our order and found a table right next to their booth, which drew looks of disdain from both of them.

We smiled.

"Funny seeing you here," I said.

"This is bordering on harassment, gentlemen," Matthews said.

"No, this would be a coincidence," I replied.

The two exchanged a look, contemplating leaving. But the waitress delivered a steaming hot, large pizza to the table. The two exchanged another glance and decided to suffer through our presence.

"Don't mind us," JD said.

Juliana's eyes flicked to Jack, flashing a cold, unimpressed gaze. "I'm sure you'll be easy to ignore."

JD's grin faded.

"Just don't pay any attention to them," Professor Matthews said. "They're looking for a reaction. Don't give them one. I've got nothing to hide. If they want to chase their tails, let them."

They peeled off slices of the gooey pizza. The smell of mozzarella, red sauce, and basil filled the air. We watched as they stuffed the piping hot pie in their mouths.

"So, are you two like an item?" JD asked.

"That's none of your business, Deputy," Juliana said.

"Isn't that against university policy?"

"There is no prohibition on relationships between faculty on equal footing. Just positions of authority."

"So, you're a thing?"

"No, we are not a thing!" Juliana wasn't doing a good job of ignoring Jack. "We are two colleagues having dinner, sharing intelligent conversation. Which is more than I can say for this exchange."

"He's trying to engage you," Evan said. "Disconnect."

Juliana looked away from JD and gazed into the professor's eyes. "You're absolutely right. Let's enjoy our meal."

We continued to stare at the table in an obnoxious way. They did their best to ignore us.

The waitress brought our pizza, and we chowed down on the cheesy, doughy goodness. It hit the spot.

Juliana and Evan finished before we did. Evan paid the tab, and the two hurried out of the restaurant.

"You two kids have a great evening," JD snarked as they passed the table.

They said nothing.

I didn't think Evan would be stupid enough to attack a colleague he'd been seen with, but I worried about Juliana nonetheless.

20

"What the hell does she see in that loser?" JD grumbled when he picked me up the next morning.

"Juliana Morgan still on your mind?" I said with a smirk.

"She can't possibly be into him, can she? The guy's a tool."

"She needs to date the singer of a rock band, right?" I teased.

His eyes narrowed at me. "I'm just saying. She could do better. And I'd hate to see her wind up like the others."

We pulled out of the parking lot and cruised down the highway. It was a nice morning, and the amber sun hovered over the horizon. Wind swirled about, and '80s rock blasted from the speakers, conjuring images of neon guitars, big hair, and music videos with cherry lipstick and fishnet stockings. Which reminded me, it was about time to make another video for the band.

We headed over to the Aegaeon and pulled into the visitors' lot. I dialed the manager from the call box, and Carol buzzed us into the lobby. We made our way to her office and grabbed a spare key to Fawn's apartment. I wanted to take a look around for clues to her disappearance.

Carol didn't hesitate in giving us the keys.

We took the elevator to the fifth floor and strolled the hallway to apartment #509. I snapped on a pair of nitrile gloves before touching the door handle. JD did the same. I inserted the key and unlocked the door. We pushed into the apartment.

There were cream walls with bleached gray hardwoods. The foyer opened to the kitchen and the living area, with a bar counter separating the two. Floor-to-ceiling sliding glass doors opened to the terrace, and the master bedroom was just off the living room. The apartment was cozy and decorated with a gray couch with teal throw pillows and carnation pink accents. Matching paintings of abstract art hung on the wall. Stainless steel appliances adorned the kitchen. It was a nice little apartment, except for the fact it had been ransacked.

The pillows had been ripped off the couch and chair. The drawers in the kitchen had been rummaged through. The mattress in the bedroom disturbed and left askew, the sheets torn off. The closet and drawers pulled apart.

Somebody was looking for something.

The bedroom had a small office area with a desk, a laptop computer, and a camera for video blogging. There were small lights and a makeshift set. I got the impression that along with her companion business, Fawn did a little private camming on the side. There were various adult novelty items around, and I figured Fawn put on a hell of a show for the guys on the Internet who paid top dollar to see her *perform*.

A fish tank near the desk bubbled, and an array of colorful fish darted through the water. If only they could talk. I figured it had been a week since they'd been fed and probably weren't far from going belly up. I moved to the aquarium and sprinkled fish food from a can near the tank. The tiny morsels speckled the top of the water. The hungry fish launched to the surface and scooped up the bits with gaping mouths.

The terrace extended to the bedroom, and the floor-to-ceiling windows offered a view of the apartment complex across the street. The rent was cheaper on this side of the building. Not much of a view.

I slid open the glass door, stepped onto the terrace from the bedroom, and looked around. I caught a glimpse of a guy in the apartment complex across the street looking at me through a telescope in his living room. He looked up from the lens as soon as I saw him—eyes round, guilt flushing his face. He quickly drew the shades.

I counted the floors up and the number of units over.

"It seems a little odd that someone would rummage through the apartment and not take the laptop, the camera, her jewelry, or other valuables," JD said. "There was no forced entry. Whoever did this had a key."

"Which they probably took from Fawn when they abducted her," I said. "I think we should pay our Peeping Tom across the street a visit. Maybe he saw something."

We left the apartment, locked up, and spoke to the property manager. I told her that the place had been disturbed and that I would send the forensics team over to dust for prints. "Please keep all maintenance personnel out of the apartment."

She didn't seem too pleased. "Well, she *is* late on the rent. I don't like to sound cold. How long do you think your investigation will continue? I'd like to get that apartment turned around and make it ready for lease."

I shrugged. "Just keep it as is for the time being."

"Whatever you say," she said with a resigned breath.

"Thank you. I know it's an inconvenience."

We left the building, walked across the street, and gained access to the neighboring building. We took the elevator up to the fifth floor, and I walked down the hallway to apartment #507 and banged on the door.

There was no reply.

I banged again and shouted, "Coconut County. We need a word with you."

Still, there was no response.

I put another heavy fist against the door and finally saw the peephole flicker. "

"How do I know you're really cops?"

I stifled a groan and flashed my badge.

"That could be fake."

"It's not fake."

"You don't look like cops."

I let JD say his favorite phrase. "We are a Special Crimes Unit."

"Bullshit," the muffled voice behind the door said.

My jaw tightened with frustration.

21

"Fine," I said. "We'll just talk through the door."

There was a long silence.

"How long have you been watching Fawn DiCarlo?"

"Who?"

"The girl whose apartment you've been peeping on."

"I'm not peeping."

"Right. That's why your telescope is aimed at her bedroom."

"No, it's not."

"Cut the shit. I saw you. I'm not concerned about that. I need to know if you saw anything unusual in her apartment. Perhaps you saw who ransacked the place."

"I didn't see anything. Like I told you, I'm not peeping on my neighbor. My telescope happened to be pointed in that direction, and I saw you two in the apartment. I thought it was odd."

"Have you seen anyone else in the apartment at any time?"

"No."

"And you never watched Fawn *perform* in her bedroom?"

"Absolutely, not."

I had no doubt he was lying.

"What's your name?"

"I don't have to tell you."

"I know your address. I'll figure it out."

He was silent again for a long moment.

"Things would be a lot easier if you cooperate. You do realize the girl you've been spying on is missing. Her leg was found in the belly of a shark at the Aquarium. We think she may be dead, and we're trying to find her killers."

He maintained his silence.

I dug into my pocket for a card and slid it under the door. "If something should jog your memory, please contact me. It's important. You could help solve a crime."

I heard him pick up the card.

"Like I said, Deputies, I haven't seen anything. I wish I could help you."

We waited another moment, but he failed to say anything else. We headed back down the hallway to the elevator and pressed the call button.

"I'm guessing that punk saw everything," JD grumbled.

The bell rang, and the door slid open. We stepped onto the elevator and plummeted down to the lobby. I called Denise as we strolled back across the street to the Aegaeon. I gave her the man's address and apartment number. With a few strokes of the keyboard, she had his name, CJ Mackey. Denise texted me his DMV photo.

Mr. Mackey was in his mid-50s. He had short curly red hair that was receding rapidly. He had a pudgy nose, a wrinkled forehead, blue eyes, and a full face. He had deep laugh lines, and his chin was beginning to sag. Kind of a geeky-looking guy. He wasn't dragging down nines and tens in the clubs. That was certain.

"Any criminal history?" I asked.

"Nope. The guy's clean. Not so much as a parking ticket."

I thanked her and ended the call.

"The guy knows something," JD said.

"He probably doesn't want it to get out that he is a pervert."

"Just look at the guy. He's got creeper written all over him."

I called Fawn DiCarlo's brother, Joe, and asked him if he wanted to take the fish in her apartment.

"Oh, man. I don't know if I can handle the responsibility."

"It's really simple. You just sprinkle fish food in."

"Yeah, but it's a pain in the ass." He paused. "Just dump them in the ocean."

"They're freshwater fish."

"Why don't you keep them?"

"The last thing I need is more pets to take care of."

"See what I'm talking about."

"Let me know if you change your mind," I said before ending the call. I looked at JD and sighed. "Let's go grab the fish tank."

He gave me a look.

"I can't just leave them there. They'll go belly up."

We went back to Fawn's apartment and evaluated the situation. It was going to be a process to move the 15-gallon tank. I didn't want to stress the fish, so I called the pet store, and they gave me the name of an aquarium mover. I gave him the details of the setup and arranged a time for the move. I used the *law enforcement card* and was able to create a sense of urgency. Corbin said he'd be right over with his helper.

I had time to kill, so I called Deputy Adams while we waited. He originally worked the Owen Ferguson disappearance. "What can you tell me about the case?"

"What do you want to know?" he asked.

"Give me your impressions."

He took a breath and thought about it. "It was some time ago, but we talked to Mr. Westwood and Ms. DiCarlo. There were no discrepancies in their stories. At that time, there was nothing to indicate foul play. If I recall correctly, the Coast Guard searched for a few days, but Owen's body never turned up."

"What did your gut tell you?"

"I go by facts, Deputy Wild. I don't shoot from the hip."

Deputy Adams and his partner, Deputy Nelson, weren't fans of ours. We weren't really fans of them either.

"I'm sure you're aware of the situation with Fawn DiCarlo."

"I am. You're more than welcome to take over the Ferguson investigation as there seems to be some overlap."

"I wouldn't want to step on your toes," I said, trying to mask my insincerity.

"My toes are just fine. Good luck, Deputy."

I ended the call.

JD's face crinkled, "You get anything useful out of him?"

"Not much."

Jack shook his head.

Adams and Nelson just collected a paycheck. They did the minimum to get by. Most of the guys in the department were solid, but there were a few bad apples in every bunch. With Flynn Westwood's massive wealth, I wouldn't be surprised if there was some kind of financial arrangement that put the investigation on the back burner.

Flynn had old money. The son of a wealthy steel magnate, the business had been in the family for generations, though Flynn was doing his best to go through it as quickly as possible. But he had the kind of wealth that even an impulsive, narcissistic man-child couldn't burn through in a lifetime.

Corbin showed up about an hour later. He and his assistant drained the tank water into a bucket with an airstone, removed the decorations and substrate, and placed them into another bucket, keeping them damp. Then they caught and transferred the fish into the bucket. I paid Corbin upfront in cash and told him to deliver the fish to *Diver Down* and set up the tank behind the bar. I asked him to call me when it was done, and I gave Teagan a heads-up.

We locked up the apartment once Corbin left, and we caught up with Mr. Westwood aboard his yacht, the *Man of Steel*. But Flynn was no Superman. Surprisingly, the boat wasn't that big. It was one of many he owned at ports across the globe.

Finished in metallic silver with sleek lines and angular features, the futuristic yacht screamed speed. With dual MTU 12V 2000 M96 engines, the 74' dream had a max speed of 44 knots. The aft deck housed an alfresco dining area. The salon was elegant with a minibar, forward helm station, and excellent views. Centerline steps led below deck to the galley and guest quarters. The foredeck was home to an oversized sun pad. A fly-bridge above with a helm station offered stunning visibility and fun in the sun. At the stern was a teak hydraulic swim platform and garage to house the tender. The metallic boat was worthy of its moniker.

We strolled across the retractable gangway to the aft deck and banged on the glass salon door.

A handsome man in his early 30s emerged from below deck. He had a slim but athletic build. His blue eyes surveyed us cautiously as he crossed the salon. I could see the outline of a pistol holstered in his waistband under his stretch-cotton navy short-sleeve button-down. The ensemble was rounded out with cream shorts and gray suede deck shoes with navy accents. A silver Oyster Perpetual Rolex adorned his wrist. It seemed to be the outfit de jure of the elite. These guys all dressed the same.

I flashed my badge, and Flynn slid open the door.

"Afternoon, gentlemen. What can I do for you?"

"Flynn Westwood?"

"That's me."

"I'm sure you've heard about Fawn DiCarlo."

"Yes. It's tragic and highly disturbing."

"When was the last time you saw Fawn?"

22

"I don't know. Maybe a month ago," Flynn said.

"Did she fall out of favor?" I asked.

"I've been keeping myself occupied with other endeavors," he said with a cocky grin.

"I'm sure you have no shortage of options."

"I'm blessed."

"How often were you seeing Fawn?"

"Whenever I felt like it."

"How often was that?"

"Sometimes once a week. Sometimes more. Sometimes less."

"But your visits had been declining lately," I said.

"Like I said, I've been pursuing other interests."

"I'm sure it was a little awkward to be around each other after Owen went missing."

Flynn's face tensed. "That was a tragedy, and I'm heart-broken about it. Owen was my best friend."

"Want to tell me a little bit about what happened?"

"I've already told the deputies everything."

"I'd like to hear it from you again."

He hesitated, staring at me with annoyed eyes. He sighed. "I'll tell you exactly what I told the others. We went out on the water for a day of sun and fun."

"Just the three of you?"

"Yes."

"That seems like an odd combination," I said. "Unless the three of you were romantically involved."

"I share a lot of things with my friends, just not my women."

"Seems to me like you were sharing Fawn with a lot of people," JD said.

Flynn's annoyed gaze found Jack. "What she did on her time was her business. When she was with me, I commanded her full attention."

"Tell me about that day," I said.

"Fawn was here from the night before. Owen stopped by, and we all had a few drinks, then decided to take the boat out for the afternoon."

"Just the three of you," I said to confirm.

"Yes, just the three of us."

"No staff. No other guests?"

"Sometimes, I like to get away and keep to myself. Having a full staff is fun at times. It can also be annoying. I'm a private person, and you have no privacy with a full-time staff."

"No bodyguards?" I asked.

"I can take care of myself."

"You're a high-profile target."

"I am. But if someone thinks they can take advantage of me, there will be a price."

"You were about to tell me what happened out on the water."

"If you'd quit interrupting me, I could tell you."

I motioned for him to proceed.

"I'll admit, we'd all had a lot to drink."

"Any drug use?"

Flynn smiled. "I'm not going to admit to a crime, Deputy."

"Any drug use?"

"We were having a good time." A guilty smile tugged his face. "Take that as you will. We had gone out to Angelfish Island. We spent the day riding jet skis, lounging on the beach, and having fun. I don't know how much you know about Fawn, but she had appetites—appetites that I was more than happy to satisfy. After all, I do like to get my money's worth. We came back to the boat, had a little fun below deck in my stateroom. When we surfaced, Owen was nowhere around."

"When was the last time you saw him?"

"He was riding a jet ski when we returned to the boat. I was distracted and not really paying attention to him."

When we returned topside, his jet ski was floating in the water, and there was no sign of him. We searched the boat. We got on a jet ski and searched the area. We looked around the island. I called the Coast Guard. They searched for days. They never found a trace of him. They think maybe he crashed, hit his head, and drowned. The current probably took him away."

"That's a good story."

"It's not a story. Owen was my best friend. I was devastated. How dare you come aboard my boat and insinuate otherwise?"

He glared at us for a moment.

"Were you guys getting along that day?"

"I think this conversation is over."

I dug into my pocket and gave him my card. With a sarcastic tone, I said, "Thanks for your cooperation."

"I've been nothing but cooperative since the incident happened. I'm more than happy to help, but I don't appreciate being accused of something."

"Nobody is accusing you of anything."

"You know, most guys in my position wouldn't say a word to you. But I've got nothing to hide."

Talking to cops was always a bad idea, even if you were innocent.

We showed ourselves across the gangway and ambled down the dock toward the parking lot.

Flynn watched us with contempt for a moment, then disappeared into the salon.

"What do you think really happened?" JD asked.

"There are three people that know the answer to that, and two of them are dead."

My mind swirled with possible scenarios. It was all just speculation at this point. Maybe it all went down just as Flynn said. Maybe Owen came to a more nefarious demise. Either way, Fawn had been in close proximity to multiple deaths, and that raised red flags.

I figured it might be a good idea to find out a little more about Ed Trammell. I was sure his widow wouldn't have good things to say about Fawn DiCarlo. But I was a little surprised by her response.

23

Ella Trammell lived in the posh neighborhood of *Stingray Bay*. Land of the perfectly manicured hedgerows and Range Rovers. Cookie-cutter McMansions full of bored housewives, spoiled kids, and nosy neighbors.

JD parked at the curb, and we strolled the walkway, past the white Lexus in the circular drive, and rang the bell. A woman's voice crackled through the speakerphone on the video doorbell. I flashed my badge and made introductions.

Ella was at the door moments later, and she seemed eager to speak with us. She was in her late 40s with blonde hair that was tinting toward gray. She wore a chocolate brown top with a cream blazer and a matching skirt. She had perfectly manicured nails and looked professional, though I'm pretty sure the woman didn't need to work. She had a round face, blue eyes, and a slightly frumpy figure. There was no doubt she had been a looker back in the day. She held onto it pretty well, but those days were gone. Though, she probably had no shortage of middle-aged suitors due to the size of her bank account.

"Are you investigating Ed's death?" Ella asked with hopeful eyes.

"We're looking into that as well as some other disappearances."

"I saw that they found that woman's leg in the belly of a shark. I can't even bring myself to say her name." She put her hand to her chest modestly and said, "I'm usually not a negative person, but that couldn't have happened to a nicer gal."

There was certainly no love lost between Ella and Fawn. I expected a degree of animosity, but I was not prepared for the level of hatred she possessed.

"I heard she was carved into tiny pieces, then fed to the shark," she said in a gleeful tone.

"We believe the leg was severed with a power tool. We haven't discovered the rest of the remains, so we are unable to say."

"I sure hope it was painful. I'd give my fortune just to have done it myself."

My brow lifted with surprise.

"Tell us how you really feel," JD snarked.

"How I really feel? I'll tell you how I really feel. That bitch killed my husband and destroyed my family. My daughter was devastated. I'm not sure Dayna will ever recover." Ella frowned. "I had a wonderful marriage to a good man."

"So good that he was seeing an escort on the side," JD muttered.

Ella's eyes blazed into him. Pure fury. The wounds were still fresh. "I don't blame Ed for being seduced by that harlot. Men have weaknesses," she said with a tight face. "I am aware of that. I'm also aware that certain dynamics of our relationship had changed. I can't compete with a woman half my age. But I can tell you this, Ed never used any drugs before he met that woman. She gave him that junk, and it killed him. And I wouldn't be surprised if she did it on purpose."

"What would she have to gain?" I asked.

Ella's eyes snapped to me and gave me a look like it was a stupid question. "Has it occurred to you that perhaps she was hired to kill my husband?"

"By whom?"

Ella shrugged. "I don't know by whom. Perhaps a business rival. A competitor. Someone who stood to benefit from the decline of Trammell-Tech Industries."

"Or maybe his ticker just gave out," JD said.

"I don't mind saying that your department has been less than helpful. That devil woman walked away from this scot-free without so much as a slap on the wrist."

"There was not enough evidence to bring charges," I said. "Fawn maintained that your husband was alive and well when she left."

Ella scoffed and rolled her eyes. "A likely story."

"It's my understanding that you filed a civil wrongful death suit."

"I did. But I'm convinced the system is entirely corrupt. The suit was dismissed. Is no one accountable for their actions anymore?"

"It seems that way at times, doesn't it?"

"Why are you here, Deputies?" she asked flatly. "I'm beginning to get the impression that you're not searching for the truth about Ed's death."

"I'm always searching for the truth, Mrs. Trammell," I said. "I'd like to know what happened to Fawn DiCarlo. That might shed some light on the bigger picture."

She took a breath, lifted her nose, and squinted at me. "I see. You're aware of my animosity toward that whore, and you think I may have had something to do with her demise."

"You did express an interest in carving her into tiny pieces."

She smiled. "Yes. And I will express that interest again. But just because I would like to do something doesn't mean I did it."

"What about your daughter?

"What about her?"

"You mentioned she took it hard."

"How else would she take it?"

24

"Does your daughter share your enthusiasm for carving Fawn up into little pieces?" I asked.

Ella's eyes narrowed at me. "So now my daughter is a suspect?"

"I'm trying to get an idea of who may have helped feed Fawn to the shark."

"Dayna had nothing to do with this. And if you think I'm going to give you any information you can use against my daughter, you're sadly mistaken."

"Does your daughter live here with you?"

"No, she does not."

"Where can I find her?"

"Figure it out for yourself."

"I will."

"I see my disappointment in your department is well justified. Good day, gentlemen."

She slammed the door in our faces, and JD and I exchanged a look. He shrugged, and we walked back to the Porsche and hopped in. Jack cranked up the engine and pulled away from the curb.

"A woman in her position could have hired someone to take care of Fawn," JD said.

"And she seems like the type to do it," I added.

I texted Denise and asked her to give me information on Ella Trammell's daughter, Dayna.

JD drove to Oyster Avenue. It was past lunchtime, and we were both looking for something to fill our bellies.

We parked at the curb, strolled the sidewalk, and ended up at *Finley McGee's*. It was a cool little spot with deck-work and life preservers on the walls. A delightful hostess seated us at a table on the sidewalk patio where we could watch the tourists wander up and down the block.

Mandy waited on us.

Jack ordered the Nacho Grande to start, and a mixed grill that contained shrimp, scallops, crab, lobster, and calamari served with rice and vegetables. I opted for a cup of clam chowder and the Havana roast pork with black beans, rice, and Cuban bread.

Jack had his head buried in his phone while we waited for our appetizers. His face twisted with a scowl. "Every gossip rag has written a story about Scarlett's little mishap."

"Any press is good press," I said, trying to put a positive spin on it.

"I don't think she needs this kind of press."

"Heard anything from her?"

"No. She ought to be getting sprung pretty soon."

"Call Joel."

"He's got enough on his plate. He doesn't need me up his ass every 15 minutes."

I pulled out my phone, put it on speaker, and called Joel. I didn't mind bothering him.

"Hey, I was just about to call," Joel said in a rush. "The system went down, so they are delayed processing inmates. I'm told it should be up in another hour or so. Hopefully, I'll get her out by late afternoon. The media is already camped out around the jail."

"Keep us posted."

"I will."

After I ended the call, Jack said, "A little time in the can might knock some sense into her."

"Maybe this was just a one-time lapse in judgment."

"Let's hope." He paused. "You know, I'm not going to be around forever. She's gonna need to look after herself one of these days."

I rolled my eyes. "You're not that old."

"Age doesn't matter. Chuck, 52, pneumonia." JD snapped his fingers. "Gone!" He frowned and shook his head. "When the man upstairs calls your number, it's over."

Mandy delivered our appetizers, and we chowed down. The chowder was full of cream and butter. Artery clogging goodness. I made short work of it and pilfered a few of JD's nachos. There were plenty to go around.

Denise called midway through the meal. "I did some digging. Dayna Trammell lists her permanent residence in Stingray Bay."

"Maybe her mother is lying. Maybe Dayna lives at home."

"I searched her social media profiles. She has a lot of cozy photos with a guy named Langston Hughes. Her timeline is full of pictures on a yacht. Langston's address listed with the DMV is *Sandpiper Point* aboard the *Sea Eye Hey*. I'm guessing that's where you'll find Dayna."

"Nice work."

"I know," she said with a smile in her voice. "And you're going to love this…"

"I'm all ears."

"Dayna repeatedly harassed Fawn on social media up until the point where Fawn blocked her. Then it looks like Dayna made additional accounts just to leave snarky comments."

"Snarky comments don't necessarily mean she was involved in Fawn's disappearance."

"I agree, but there were several thinly veiled threats. *You're going to get what's coming to you. I know people.*"

"People say that shit all the time," I said. "But it does make her a person of interest."

I thanked Denise for the info and ended the call. We finished the meal, and Jack paid the tab. We headed back to Sandpiper Point and looked for the *Sea Eye Hey*. It was a nice starter yacht, bought and paid for by his father. A 70' Monaco with a striking silhouette, a fly-bridge with a hardtop and helm station, and a salon with accordion-style glass doors that allowed seamless blending of indoor and outdoor spaces. Side decks led to the foredeck with large sun-pads. A moulded hardtop covered the aft deck and alfresco dining area.

Langston and Dayna lounged on the aft deck as we arrived. Theirs was a life of leisure, 24/7.

I flashed my badge and made introductions as we crossed the gangway to the aft deck.

"My mother called. Said you'd probably be stopping by to harass me," Dayna grumbled.

Dayna was an attractive blonde in her early 20s. She wore a royal blue, off-the-shoulder sundress and a pearl necklace. She had thin lips and a narrow jaw. She resembled her mother and had a perpetual look of annoyance on her face.

Langston had caramel brown hair that was trimmed on the sides and longer on top. He had a strong jaw, square chin, and a flat nose. Kinda ruff around the edges for a trust-fund baby. His narrow blue eyes were perched between high cheekbones and a strong brow. He had a muscular physique, and his cocky, arrogant demeanor permeated the air without saying a word.

"You made some pretty nasty remarks on social media," I said.

"What do you expect? She killed my father. I think I'm entitled to say a few nasty things. Am I supposed to just let that slide and say, *'Oh well, shit happens?'*"

25

"Y ou don't have to talk to these people, you know that?" Langston said.

"I know," Dayna replied. "I'm not talking to them. But I think it's appalling that they'd have the nerve to come here and question me in regard to that bitch's death."

"We're just trying to get a look at the bigger picture," I said.

"I don't see how her death has anything to do with me," Dayna said. "Are you continuing to investigate my father's death?"

"We believe Fawn disappeared from her apartment complex last Thursday evening," I said, ignoring her.

"I was here with Langley," she said in a triumphant tone. "So you can take us off your suspect list."

"Langston, Langley, CIA," I said. "I get it."

"It's a nickname my friends gave me. It kind of stuck. Seemed like a fitting name for the boat."

"So, you were both here Thursday evening. All evening? And you don't know anything about her abduction?"

"That's correct," Dayna replied.

I dug into my pocket and tossed my card onto the table. "There's more than one death tied to this case. If you can think of anything helpful, please contact me."

"Yeah, we'll get right on that," Langston said in an insincere tone.

This was going nowhere, so we left the boat and strolled the dock toward the parking lot. My phone buzzed with a call from Joel. I swiped the screen and put it to my ear. "Tell me good news."

"Operation jailbreak is a success. She's out. Want to talk to her? She's right here."

"Put her on the phone."

The car noise rumbled through the speakerphone as Joel handed his device to Scarlett.

"How pissed off is Jack?" she asked.

"He's not happy."

JD eyed me and held out his hand. I gave him the phone. "Is this what success looks like? There's a picture of your mugshot on every gossip website across the net. You look like shit."

"I just spent 24 hours in a crappy jail cell with some really stinky people. I'm tired, smelly, and hungry. You think you could lay off for just a bit?"

"It's your life. Live it how you want."

"Look, I had one drink at a party. Which I haven't done in over a year. I wasn't drunk."

"LAPD seems to think you were drunk."

"I was barely over the limit. It was a strong drink. Maybe I didn't realize how strong."

"You shouldn't have gotten into the car."

"Pfft, you're one to talk."

"My mugshot isn't all over the Internet."

"That's not why I crashed. A dog darted into the street, and I swerved to avoid it. What was I supposed to do?"

"Take a cab. A limousine. You can afford it."

"You're not really one to lecture me. You drink all the time. It's practically in your job description. And don't get me started about how many times you've wrecked the Porsche."

"I've never wrecked the Porsche. Tyson wrecked the Porsche. All the other stuff just happened."

"Look, I regret this whole thing. If I could go back in time and not have that drink, I would. The studio wants me to go to rehab, even though I don't think I have a problem. Joel's gonna hook me up with a good lawyer. I know I screwed up. What I need is your support. I don't need you yelling at me."

"I'm not yelling at you. Have I raised my voice?"

"No, but you have that tone."

"I'm sorry, I didn't realize I was supposed to be excited about this."

She sighed. "You're insufferable."

"I'm insufferable? That's rich."

"Goodbye, Jack," she droned, then ended the call.

Jack was about to blow a fuse. "She just hung up on me," he said in disbelief.

He instantly redialed Joel. "We must have gotten cut off."

"We're going through the canyons now," Joel said. "I'll have her call you back later."

JD grumbled and handed the phone to me, steam coming from his ears.

"I think everybody needs a little time to cool off," I said.

"Everything's under control, don't worry," Joel assured. "I talked to Susan, and so far, *Ultra Mega 3* is moving forward, but definitely getting delayed a few weeks. The whole rehab thing is largely a PR move. Scarlett will have to make a few public statements, express remorse, blah, blah, blah. Then production will begin. But if she has one screw-up during that time frame, they will drop her." He said it to me and to her. "So, believe me, we all have an incentive to see Scarlett on the straight and narrow."

"It was an accident," she muttered in the background. "It could have happened to anyone."

"We'll talk more later," Joel said before ending the call.

Jack took a deep breath and tried to calm down. The redness faded from his face, and the veins started to settle. His temples weren't pulsing as much. "I'm just going to absolve myself of this. It's not my issue. She's an adult. Getting mad about it isn't going to change anything."

"I'm impressed. That's very Zen of you."

"I am a calm, Zen master." He said, turning up his palms, holding his thumb and index finger together in a serene manner, mimicking the enlightened.

Paris called as we climbed into the Porsche. "Hey, I've got a favor to ask."

26

"Do you think Jack would be willing to speak on camera about Scarlett's recent arrest?" Paris asked.

I laughed. "Absolutely not. I don't think you want to get anywhere near him right now."

"I understand it must be very upsetting for him," she said, trying to sound empathetic. Empathy wasn't one of her stronger qualities.

"Just leave it be."

"But it's a national news story with a local angle. We could spin it into a positive piece about addiction and overcoming challenges."

"No."

She sighed. "What are you, his manager?"

"Yes."

"I'd like to hear it straight from the horse's mouth."

I held the phone to Jack. "Tell her no."

He leaned into the phone. "No."

I put it back to my ear. "There you go."

"I'll remember that next time you need a favor from me."

"Is that a threat?"

"You scratch my back, Deputy, I scratch yours."

"Goodbye, Paris."

"Goodbye, Deputy."

I ended the call. JD cranked up the engine, and we pulled out of the parking lot. We headed to *Mega Music* to grab speaker cables. The cable to one of the PA speakers was shorting out and crackling.

The place was a musician's dream. They stocked every imaginable music-related item. Guitars of every shape, size, and color hung from racks on the walls. Rows and rows of amplifiers and speaker cabinets lined the showroom floor. There was a drum section with kits, cymbals, sticks, and drum heads. The recording section had mixing consoles and studio speakers, high-end condenser microphones, and the DJ section had stage lights and fog machines. The keyboard section had everything from small portable 21-key units up to fully weighted 88-key controllers and synthesizers.

There was always some kid banging incessantly on a drum kit or somebody scratching out a terrible cover of a guitar solo. Employees seemed immune to it all.

We made our way to the PA section, and JD perused the rack of speaker cables, looking for the right connectors. He grabbed a couple and took them to the register.

There were a couple kids playing high-end Les Pauls. $3,000 guitars with flame maple tops. After a few licks, they unplugged the guitars and took them up toward the register. As they got close, they bolted out the door with the instruments. Wearing baseball caps pulled low and dark sunglasses, their faces were somewhat obscured from security cameras.

The clerk behind the counter shouted at them, and I took off running. I chased them into the parking lot. They hopped into the side door of a white cargo van, and the vehicle took off, tires squealing. I chased after it to no avail. It screeched around the corner, barreling down the lane, then pulled out onto the main roadway. The vehicle didn't have any plates.

I called Denise at the station and alerted her. "Put out a BOLO on a white cargo van and send a patrol unit to Mega Music to take a statement."

I walked back inside and rejoined JD at the checkout counter.

"You catch them?" the clerk asked.

I shook my head.

"Bummer."

"This kind of thing happen a lot?"

"It's happening more frequently. It started with small stuff. Cables, strings, picks. They just keep getting more brazen.

They'll take anything that's not bolted down. We try to keep the high-dollar stuff away from the exit, but you know, we get busy in here. It's hard to keep tabs on what people are doing."

I told him a patrol unit would be by to take a statement.

He seemed indifferent about the whole thing. He was just an hourly employee. He didn't have to eat the $6,000-worth of guitars that just went out the door.

With any luck, the instruments would turn up in a local pawn shop.

We stepped outside into the bright sun and walked to the Porsche. The van was long gone. We climbed in and drove to the practice studio in the warehouse district.

The usual group of miscreants hung out by the entrance, drinking beer and smoking cigarettes. They high-fived JD as we entered. We made our way down the dim corridor, and Jack's keys jingled as he unlocked the door to the practice space. We stepped inside, and there was an envelope on the floor. Someone had slid it under the door. JD stepped over it, and I snatched it up.

It was addressed to *Thrash*.

"Looks like you got fan mail," I said.

"Open it."

He unpackaged the cables, disconnected the old ones, and replaced them with new ones while I tore into the envelope. I pulled out the handwritten letter and began reading. My eyes misted about halfway through. I finished the letter and said, "You might want to take a look at this."

27

I gave the letter to Jack. It didn't take long for his eyes to turn slick too. He wiped the corners with the back of his hand.

"What are you going to do?" I asked.

"What do you think I'm going to do?"

He folded the letter and stuffed it back into the envelope. We locked up and headed back outside. He displayed the letter to the miscreants, waving it about. "Anybody see who left this?"

They all exchanged dumb looks.

"No, man."

"Dude, some lady came by. She didn't stay long."

"That's right. I forgot."

They were all stoned out of their minds. The days ran together, each one the same.

"What happened? Somebody make a death threat?"

They all chuckled.

JD scowled at them. The letter was no laughing matter.

"If you see a couple of new, signature Les Pauls, one in Anaconda green and the other in Vermillion, let me know," I said.

"What happened? You guys get ripped off again?"

"No. Mega Music."

"Fuck that place. Overpriced big box shop."

"This just makes prices go up. Gotta come from somewhere."

"We'll let you know if we see anything," another kid said.

We left the gang and hopped into the Porsche.

"I don't know about you, but it's gotta be getting close to happy hour," JD said.

We had a little time to kill before band practice, and we ended up at *Wetsuit* on the strip. JD ordered the crab cakes and sliders for appetizers to cushion the whiskey. We sipped our beverages, snacked, and soaked up the delightful views of svelte waitresses in tight neoprene tops and bikini bottoms. I fell in love every time we came here.

The crab cakes didn't last long. I think I was on my second glass of whiskey when my phone buzzed with an *unknown call*. I swiped the screen and answered. A soft female voice asked, "Deputy Wild?"

"You got him."

"I called the Sheriff's Department. They told me you were the lead investigator on the Fawn DiCarlo case."

"That's correct. How can I help you?"

"I heard you interviewed Dayna Trammell. Is she a person of interest?"

"I can't comment on that."

"Well, she should be."

"Is that so?" She had my full attention.

"She repeatedly bragged about wanting to have Fawn killed."

I played devil's advocate. "What people say and what people do are often two different things."

"Yes, but Dayna can be ruthless. I've never known the girl not to follow through. And Langston is a creep. He knows shady characters."

"And what is your connection to Dayna and Langston?"

She hesitated a moment, then coyly said, "I'm a *friend*."

"A friend?" I said, mirroring her. I appreciated the tip, but with friends like that, who needed enemies.

"Let's just say we run in the same social circles. And news travels fast."

"Apparently so."

"I'm sure you get a lot of tips, and you probably think I'm crazy. But I know for a fact what Langston is capable of. He doesn't have the balls to commit murder himself, but he's not beyond hiring someone to do it."

"And what makes you so sure of that?"

"Because he hired a hitman to kill Keira Bell."

That hung there for a moment.

"And who is Keira Bell?"

"She was my best friend."

"I'm sorry for your loss. Do you have anything to back up these accusations?"

"Keira had accused Langston of sexual misconduct. Then she turned up dead. How convenient for him. Without a witness, the charges were dropped."

"And how did your friend die?"

She groaned. "Don't dismiss this."

"I'm not dismissing anything. I asked you a simple question."

She huffed. "The official report is that she OD'd on a combination of sleeping pills and acetaminophen."

"She committed suicide," I said.

"She did not commit suicide. She was murdered. And it was set up to make it look like a suicide. But I swear to you, Keira was not suicidal. She had just met this new guy. She was on cloud nine. She had no intention of ending her life."

"You never know what's going on inside. Some people put on a good front."

She growled into the phone. "Keira was not putting on a good front. Why won't anyone listen to me?"

"What's your name?"

"I'm not telling you my name."

"I can find out."

"What does it matter, anyway?"

"If everything you say is true, an anonymous source isn't going to cut it. I need a sworn statement, and even then, it's just a hunch."

"It's not a hunch. It's a fact."

"Maybe. But neither you nor I can prove it."

She huffed again. "You know, you're really pissing me off."

I chuckled. "I apologize if I've upset you. But I need something solid. I'll make some phone calls, check out a few facts, then I'll get back in touch with you. Is there a number where I can reach you at? Your number showed up as unknown."

"I'll call you back in 15 minutes."

I rolled my eyes. "Fine. At least give me a name in the meantime that I can refer to you as."

She paused. "Amanda. You can call me Amanda."

It clearly wasn't her name.

I ended the call and dialed Denise. "What can you tell me about Keira Bell?"

28

"Official cause of death was an overdose," Denise said. "Medical examiner in Pineapple Bay ruled it a suicide. Apparently, she had just moved from Coconut Key."

"When did this happen?"

"A few months ago."

"What about the sexual assault charges?"

"Prosecutor dropped the charges against Langston after her death."

"And the alleged assault took place here in Coconut Key?"

"According to Keira's statement," Denise said. "Think there could be some truth to your tipster?"

"I guess we'll have to find out." I thanked her and ended the call.

I dialed Isabella and asked her to track the unknown number that called my phone.

"That number belongs to Andrea Logan." She texted me the digits. "Need anything else?"

"Pull the phone records for Keira Bell as well as Dayna Trammell and Langston Hughes. Check Dayna's and Langston's bank accounts for unusual transactions." I filled her in on the situation.

"That's going to take a little digging, but I'll get around to it."

"Let me know when you've got something."

"Will do."

I ended the call and dialed Andrea Logan. She didn't sound too pleased. "How did you get this number?"

"I have ways."

"Did you call your people? Check things out?"

"I'm looking into it. Why did Keira move to Pineapple Bay?"

"She needed to get away."

"I wouldn't really call Pineapple Bay *getting away.*"

"Sometimes, all you need is a little distance. She didn't want to run into Langston at the usual clubs. I'm telling you, he had her killed."

"Do you know who he hired?"

"That's your job. Use your *ways*," she snarked.

"I'll be in touch."

"Keep my name out of it. The last thing I need is that guy coming after me."

"I'll keep your name out of it, but there may come a time when you will need to testify."

"Just arrest that guy and get him behind bars where he belongs."

She ended the call, and I slipped the phone back into my pocket. I caught JD up to speed, though he'd heard most of it.

It was nearing time for band practice. We finished our drinks, stuffed the rest of the appetizers in our mouths, and left *Wetsuit*. Someone had posted flyers with Fawn's picture on light poles and in store windows, asking for anyone who had any information about her disappearance to call a number. There were pull-off tabs. The number belonged to JC Egan. Maybe he really did care for Fawn. Or maybe he was just trying to make himself look good.

We headed back to the warehouse district for band practice. I called Keira Bell's mom, Charlotte, and told her I was doing a follow-up investigation on the case. She pretty much told me what Andrea had said—that Keira was in a good frame of mind. Not depressed. She thought it was totally out of character for her daughter to commit suicide.

"What about the new guy she was dating?"

"She never mentioned anything to me," Charlotte said. "I told all the stuff to the investigators at the time. Everybody was convinced she killed herself. I told them there was no way that she'd do that. I've had plenty of conversations with Andrea about this."

"What do you make of her theory?"

"Her theory is about as good as any other theory. I think Andrea can be a bit dramatic at times, but she would know what was going on in Keira's life better than anyone." She paused, and a deep sigh exhaled her lungs. "I sure hope you find the truth, Deputy."

"We'll do our best. I'll let you know if I discover anything."

"Please do."

I ended the call about the time we pulled into the parking lot. There were considerably more cars in the lot than before. The miscreants were still out front. We hopped out of the vehicle, high-fived the guys, and pushed into the dim hallway. The rest of the band had already arrived and was tuning up. Wild Fury ran through their set, noodled around with a few new ideas, and we all ended up at *Gingerbread's* afterward. It was just a few blocks off-campus.

It wasn't our usual hangout, but I dug the place. JD was pushing for it for some reason. It was a cozy little pub with every imaginable draft beer, a wide selection of wine, and of course, whiskey. There were dartboards, pool tables, and an eclectic mix of students and professors.

As soon as we stepped inside, I knew why JD wanted to come here.

29

I groaned. "Are you stalking her?"

"I'm not stalking her," JD said. "I may happen to follow her on social media. She posted that she was here, and I wanted to make sure she survived last night."

"If she posted on social media, she clearly survived."

Jack frowned at me and headed to the bar.

Juliana Morgan was at the back of the club, bending over a pool table. She had a nice bend. She was with a friend. A rather attractive female friend.

I couldn't blame JD for his newly acquired infatuation with the occult studies professor. She was quite enthralling.

Jack ordered a round of drinks for us all. Hayden, the bartender, served us a heavy pour, and Jack lifted his glass to toast. "To rock 'n' roll."

We clinked glasses and sipped the fine whiskey.

Reese, the cute little waitress that I had been trying to connect with, was still out of town. The recent events had left her quite frazzled. I wasn't sure if she would ever come back to Coconut Key.

JD asked Hayden to send over another round for the ladies at the pool table and a round of whiskey for us. With his eyes on the target, Jack puffed up and started toward Juliana.

The clack of the cue ball rang out, rock 'n' roll filtered from the jukebox, and the smell of pipe smoke wafted in from the patio.

"This will give me an opportunity to win back some of that money you stole from me," JD muttered along the way.

"You lost fair and square."

He dismissed the notion. A wide grin tugged his face as we arrived at the tables. There were two, side by side. "Good evening, ladies."

Juliana stifled a groan and shot him a cold stare. She lined up her shot, drew the stick back, and tapped the cue ball. It rolled across the felt and clacked the two-ball, cutting it into the side pocket, clean. She had a nice stroke. "Shouldn't you be out solving a mystery?"

"Just recharging the batteries," JD said. "Can't work all the time."

"I think you two hardly work at all."

The waitress arrived with a tray of beverages and dealt them out.

Juliana looked confused. "We didn't order those. We were just leaving after this game."

The waitress smiled. "Complements of Deputy Donovan."

Jack smiled. "You're not gonna turn down a free drink, are you?"

"I'm not," Juliana's friend said, taking the beverage.

Juliana shot her an annoyed glance.

"Since Juliana doesn't have any manners, allow me to introduce myself... Jack Donovan, and this is my partner, Tyson Wild."

"It's a pleasure to meet you both. My name is Catalina, but my friends call me Cat... or Kitty... " she smirked, and her sultry eyes targeted me. "And if you're really lucky, I might let you see my—"

"Cat!" Juliana scolded.

"Is she always this annoying?" JD asked.

"Sometimes she needs to be reminded how to have fun," Cat said.

"I know how to have fun," Juliana assured. "And I was doing that before these two arrived."

Cat whispered, "She just needs to get laid."

"Cat!"

"Just saying."

"You'll have to excuse her," Juliana said. "She has no filter."

"Why filter anything?" Cat asked. "Life's too short not to say what you mean and mean what you say."

"Exactly!" JD said with a grin.

Cat smiled back at him.

She was gorgeous. Jet black hair with creamy skin and sky blue eyes. She had all the right parts in all the right places, and the skimpy red dress could barely contain them. She inspired a quick pulse and could make most men trip over their words.

"And why doesn't she like you two?" Cat asked.

"Oh, she likes us," JD said. "She's just afraid to admit it."

Juliana pretended to ignore us and lined up another shot.

"Well, she's a poor judge of character because I'm beginning to like you two already."

"You've got good taste."

Juliana struck the cue ball.

This time she missed.

"Yay! I get a turn." Cat bounced up and down.

I liked her bounce. I liked it a lot.

Cat chalked her cue and lined up her shot. She arched over the table, her delightful mounds of cleavage dangling above the felt.

JD and I tried not to stare. We failed miserably.

Cat drew the stick back and struck the cue ball with a horrible sound—that thin, off-center plink that shuddered the stick and your forearm. The ball veered off to the side, missing the target completely. Cat wasn't going to win any tournaments, but she looked good doing it.

Cat didn't seem too upset by her poor performance. She shrugged it off and took another sip of her drink, her lipstick staining the glass.

"I'm trying to let you win, but you gotta work with me," Juliana said.

Cat wiggled her drink. "She'd be in trouble if I was sober."

Juliana rolled her eyes and lined up another shot.

Cat seemed more interested in us than the game anyway. She wouldn't get any complaints from me. She leaned in and whispered, "I missed on purpose."

I gave her a wink and a nod, going along with it.

"So, are you guys good cops or bad cops?"

"They are bad cops," Juliana muttered.

"Oooh, that sounds exciting," she said with a naughty gleam in her eyes.

30

"So, what are you two sleuths working on now?" Cat asked.

"They're working on ruining an innocent man's life," Juliana quipped.

"The Coed Killer," JD said.

"And you think he could be a member of the faculty?"

"They're wrong," Juliana said.

"We're keeping all possibilities open," I said.

Cat's eyes flicked to me. "Sounds intriguing." Her eyes darted back to JD. "Why do you look so familiar to me?"

"Do you like rock 'n' roll?"

She gasped, and her eyes widened with recognition. "You're the singer for Wild Fury."

JD smiled. "And the rest of the band is right over there," he said, motioning back to the bar.

"You know, I think you two are the most interesting of all Juliana's friends."

"They're not my friends," Juliana said, sinking another ball.

"You really have to teach her some manners," JD muttered to Cat.

"I'm trying to get her out more. She always has her nose buried in a demonology book, or she's conversing with stuffy colleagues who wouldn't know a good time if it hit them in the face."

"I happen to like my stuffy colleagues and a more cerebral form of entertainment."

Cat shrugged and sipped her drink. "Me, I'm all about the simple pleasures. Give me good friends, good music, and smooth whiskey, and I'm happy."

"A woman after my own heart," JD said.

Juliana took another stroke and sank the eight-ball with a satisfying clunk. She stood up triumphantly and set her cue stick on the table. "Thanks for the drink, gentlemen, but I believe it's time we should be going." She looked at her watch. "I've got an early class to teach in the morning."

"You're going to miss all the fun," JD said. "We are about to go back to the boat for a little after-party. I can run it by the guys in the band, and if they think you're cool enough, we might let you come along."

"Of course we're cool enough." Cat smiled.

Juliana rolled her eyes. "Your silly little mind games are not going to work with me. I'm not one of your impressionable young groupies." She motioned to the plethora of college-age women in the bar. "I'm sure you'll have no shortage of takers tonight."

"After-party on the boat sounds like fun," Cat said. She looked at Juliana. "Maybe you should loosen up."

Juliana took her friend by the arm. "Sorry, gentlemen. Cat's coming home with me. I can't allow her to make poor life decisions."

"But I like poor life decisions."

Juliana dragged her friend away. Cat looked over her shoulder at us and waved, her eyes smoldering.

"Are we just going to let them walk away?" JD muttered.

"Don't chase. Never chase."

I smiled and waved back at Cat, watching her hips sway from side to side.

"Rack'em up," JD said. "I'm going to win my money back."

I dropped a few quarters into the slot, and the balls rolled free. I racked them and let JD break after he selected a cue stick.

"Are you good? Are you sure it's not bent?" I teased. "Maybe you should check the table, make sure it's level."

He scowled at me.

"No excuses this time."

"I don't need an excuse to whoop your ass."

He lined up the shot and broke. The cue ball smacked the one-ball with a loud crack, and the rest scattered. They bounced off the bumpers, and the six-ball dropped into a pocket.

A sly grin tugged on JD's face.

Maybe he was bringing his *A-game.*

31

Two big guys with leather vests, boots, horseshoe mustaches, and rockabilly sideburns started knocking balls around the table next to us. They smelled like whiskey, oil, and the open road, mixed with a day or two of body odor.

They weren't the usual type you'd see in a place like *Gingerbread's*. They were looking for trouble.

One had rusty red hair, the other jet-black hair that curled to his shoulders.

The rocker on the back of their vests read *Savage Barbarians*. I'd had run-ins with the Barbarians before. Quite a few of their members were currently serving long stretches. I didn't recognize these fellas. According to the patch on their vests, they were from a different chapter. Not local.

I didn't pay them much attention at first. If they stayed in their lane, I'd stay in mine.

At $20 a rack, it didn't take long for JD to get $100 in the hole.

"Double or nothing," Jack said, his face tense and his cheeks reddening with frustration.

"Are you sure you want to go down that road?" I asked.

He snarled at me. "Rack 'em."

I dropped more quarters into the slot and racked the balls. I let JD break.

He struck the cue ball with fierce determination. It rocketed across the felt and sent the rack of balls scattering across the table. He dropped a solid in one pocket and a stripe in another. He had his pick, and after a moment's contemplation, he decided on stripes.

I don't know what happened. Either he got lucky, or he'd had enough drinks that he was starting to shoot straight. He ran the table. With each ball that fell into a pocket, JD grew more confident. He pranced around the felt like he was the greatest pool player in the world. And for that moment, he might well have been.

He lined up the eight-ball. It was a relatively straightforward shot. The ball leaned against the bumper. JD would have to kiss it just right with the cue-ball to get it to roll down the bumper into the corner pocket.

"That's a tough shot," I said, trying to get in his head. It wasn't that difficult. "Don't scratch."

"I am unshakable," JD said as he drew the cue stick back. Just as he completed his stroke, the burly dude at the other table bent over to line up his shot. He bumped JD's cue, sending it awry. Jack clinked the cue-ball, sending it off in an unwanted direction. It kissed off another ball and went into the side pocket.

Needless to say, JD wasn't a happy camper. "Hey, Bud. Watch what you're doing. I got money on this game."

The biker towered over JD. He looked over his shoulder. "You say something?"

JD was not about to back down. "You messed up my shot. You cost me $200 bucks.

"Life's a bitch, ain't it?"

"It's not a big deal," I said. "Just do it over. We'll put the balls back where they were."

JD's face tensed, and the burly red-haired dude went back to his shot. He muttered, "Listen to your bitch-ass friend."

It was the wrong thing to say.

Now *my* blood started to percolate.

JD wasn't about to have any of it. He bumped the biker's cue stick just as he took a shot, sending his cue in the wrong direction. "Oops, my bad."

The burly dude stood tall, clenched his cue stick tight. Without a second thought, Red swung it around, back-handing it toward JD. The stick slashed the air, careening toward Jack's jaw.

I watched the whole thing go down in slow motion, cringing, hoping Jack still had his reaction time after the copious amounts of alcohol.

JD ducked, and the cue stick whooshed over his head.

Jack countered with a hard right to the biker's belly, doubling him over. A groan tensed Red's face. He swung the cue back around.

Jack blocked the biker's arm, then launched an upper that connected with the dick-head's jaw.

Red had a chin of steel. JD's fist knocked his head back, but the biker recovered quickly. He shrugged it off, looked down at Jack, and snarled.

That's when JD's eyes rounded, and he realized he may have bitten off more than he could chew.

While that went down, the biker's buddy grabbed a ball from the table and launched toward me, his meaty fingers wrapped around a yellow nine-ball.

He swung a hard right for my jaw.

His loaded fist careened through the air.

I blocked his swing with my right, pushing his arm aside, grabbing his wrist. I threw a hard left into his ribs.

Jet crumpled around my fist, then spun around with his back facing me and launched his left elbow toward my nose while I still clasped his right wrist.

He was a spry bastard for his size.

I blocked the elbow and kicked the back of his knee, crumpling him to the ground. In a fluid motion, I pulled my cuffs from a cargo pocket and slapped them around his right wrist, which I still had hold of. Once the cuff was latched, my right hand was free to grab a fistful of his hair. I smashed his face into the edge of the pool table.

Blood spewed from his nose.

With a growl, he sprang to his feet and bucked me off his back.

I flew back against the felt, and the behemoth spun around and charged me, his face red like a demon, my cuffs dangling from his right wrist.

32

There wasn't much room between the pool tables. The deathmatch took place in the back of the bar in the corner. Not much room to move around. It favored the big guys. You couldn't dance around and wear out your opponent.

A crowd had gathered. They always do.

As civilized as we've become, people will still watch spectacles of competition and carnage. They'd line up to watch people fed to lions if it was legal.

Unfazed by the uppercut, Red responded.

He threw a sledgehammer left toward Jack's jaw and connected. It twisted him around, twirling his long blond hair. He fell against the pool table then tumbled to the ground.

"Enough, gentlemen," a nerdy professor shouted. "You're better than this. I demand you stop this toxic behavior now!"

Red scoffed, grabbed a billiard ball from the table, and hurled it at the scrawny man. It cracked him in the head, and he tumbled back into the crowd.

If anyone else had any ideas of intervening, that squashed the thought.

Jet stomped toward me, and I kicked him in the belly. He tumbled back against the other table. I grabbed a pool cue as the demon sprang back toward me. I swung with all my might and cracked the stick across the side of his skull. It split in two, and the narrow end went tumbling away.

It paused him for a moment.

Maybe he was too drunk to really feel it, but he charged at me. My momentum had carried me forward, so I was at a bad angle and exposed.

The demon swung a hard left hook that connected with my right cheekbone. The force twisted me to the side.

He followed with a hard right, and I ducked under his meaty fist. It swished overhead, the handcuffs dangling around his arm rattled.

I jabbed the end of the pool cue into his rib cage, and that got his attention. I followed with a hard left hook of my own. It felt like pounding a concrete wall. It paused him long enough for me to come back with a hard swing, raking the pool cue across the bridge of his already busted nose. That tilted his head back, and he clutched at his face with both hands.

While that went down, Red pounced on JD. He grabbed him by his shirt and flung him through the air. Jack crashed atop a nearby table, spilling drinks, sending glasses tumbling to the ground, shattering into thousands of tiny shards. JD flopped over the tabletop and smacked the concrete on the other side.

He sprang to his feet near the dartboard and grabbed a handful of darts. He hurled them at Red.

The big guy ducked and dodged and continued his relentless march toward JD. One of the darts stuck into his forearm. He picked it out and tossed it aside. All it did was piss him off further.

JD flashed his shiny gold badge, but Red didn't give two shits about that.

The two circled each other around the toppled table.

Red flung the table aside and charged JD like a snarling bull, launching a sweeping right.

Jack sidestepped, spun around, and put a good shot into Red's kidney as he passed.

The two squared off again.

"You squirrelly little fuck," Red growled.

He charged JD again and tackled him into the wall. The wall had a drink ledge that carved into JD's back. It had to hurt.

A neon beer sign fell down and shattered on the concrete. Shards scattered and crunched underfoot.

Red had JD against the ropes, pummeling heavy body-blows.

Jack did his best to protect himself. Body shots will take it out of you and leave you short of breath. And these weren't the kind of body shots JD liked.

He kicked the bastard in the shin, and Red's face crinkled with pain. He responded by launching a hard right toward Jack's face.

JD ducked.

Red's fist smacked the wall, shattering his knuckles. He grimaced with pain.

JD spun away, grabbed a stick from a rack on the wall, and swung for Red's face. He whacked the dirt-ball upside the head as hard as he could.

That certainly got Red's attention.

The cue stick splintered, and the ogre saw stars.

He shook his head and blinked his eyes, then gathered his wits. His face twisted into a snarl as he marched toward JD, pushing him into the corner.

This guy could take a beating and keep coming.

33

The big bastard closed in, and JD readied for the onslaught.

The guys in the band rushed in and mauled Red. Like hornets, they swarmed and stung with punches and kicks.

The dirtbag tossed them off like fleas. The skinny rockers were no match for a hardcore bruiser like Red.

By that time, I'd finished Jet and had him cuffed.

I launched across the pool table and tackled the Red. We crashed into the wall, and I took him down to the ground. We wrestled on the concrete, sweat dripping onto the floor. His stench filled my nostrils. I got the ogre in a chokehold, and his face reddened. The veins in his temples bulged.

He fought it for a moment, but the restriction of blood and air didn't take long. A matter of seconds.

Red tapped out before things went dark.

He gasped for breath when I released him.

I wrenched his arm behind his back, and JD tossed me his cuffs. I slapped the hard metal around Red's thick wrists.

Somebody had called the sheriff's department, and Deputies Erickson and Faulkner pushed through the crowd to see the chaos just as I caught my breath. My heart pounded, and sweat misted my brow.

The two thugs groaned.

"What the hell happened here?" Erickson asked.

"They started it," JD said, like a scolded child.

Erickson rolled his eyes.

The deputies yanked the scumbags to their feet and escorted them out of *Gingerbread's*.

"Dude, that was totally fucking awesome," Crash said.

I rolled my eyes.

"You guys stomped them."

"Thanks for the backup," JD said, even though they didn't do much.

"One for all, and all for one. Wild Fury for life!" Crash said.

The crowd of onlookers dissipated, and the guys helped us clean up the mess.

EMTs and paramedics arrived and tended to the professor who got hit with the billiard ball. He was okay, but he had a welt the size of a softball on his forehead. I can't imagine he felt too good. The EMTs convinced him to go to the emergency room for an evaluation and a CT scan. I was pretty sure he was going to sue me, JD, the bikers, the bar, and the department.

A waitress swept up the broken glass from the neon sign, and we told Hayden we'd pay for any damages and buy new pool cues. They were all warped anyway. We told him to go ahead and replace the felt on the pool tables and have them leveled. They needed it.

He poured us another round and fixed us up with bags of ice for our sore faces. "You think you guys could put on a show like that every weekend? Hell, I'll sell tickets."

We laughed.

"Once a week might be a little too often," JD said, shifting his sore jaw from side to side. "I need a little more recovery time."

"You still owe me $200 bucks," I said, teasing him.

JD's face crinkled. "What!?"

"You lost, fair and square," I said.

He scowled at me. "It wasn't fair and square. Circumstances beyond my control."

"How about we settle this with one game, $200—winner takes all."

JD frowned. "Not tonight. I still have a little double vision."

I rolled my eyes. "A likely story."

We finished our drinks, left Hayden a generous tip, and went back to the *Avventura* with the band. They had rounded up a couple of prospects, and the party continued until the wee hours of the morning.

I retired early, tired and sore.

Daniels called first thing in the morning and barked through the speaker, "What's this I hear about a bar fight?"

"We were assaulted. I identified myself as a police officer, and the suspects did not comply with commands to cease and desist."

Daniels grumbled under his breath, then said, "This is a stupid question, but how much had you two been drinking?"

"You're right. That's a stupid question."

"And how exactly did this start?"

I gave him the details.

"So, JD started this?"

"No, JD responded to a situation."

"You mean he provoked a situation."

"Well, it's all a matter of perspective."

"At least you didn't shoot anybody." He sighed. "I'm not too keen on this going to trial and having you two nitwits cross-examined. The department's under enough scrutiny as it is. Right now, these thugs are looking at aggravated assault and battery of a law enforcement officer, among other things. You want to proceed with this?"

I exhaled a deep breath. "Cut them loose."

I didn't want to let them walk, but Daniels was right. This thing could blow up and reflect negatively.

"Keep him on a short leash," Daniels said in reference to JD.

I chuckled. "Sure thing."

I ended the call and set the phone back on the nightstand. My face was still sore from Jet's fist. I wiped the sleep from my eyes and pulled myself out of bed. The morning sun blasted through the cracks in the blinds. I took a shower, then ambled down to the galley to make breakfast. I figured the rest of the guys wouldn't be up too early this morning. I put on a pot of coffee and scrambled eggs.

Paris Delaney called. I cringed when I saw her name on the caller ID. I figured she had gotten word of our little adventure and was going to blast it out to all her followers. Exactly what Daniels didn't want to happen. I swiped the screen and put the phone to my ear. "I don't know what you heard, but we didn't start the situation."

"What situation?"

I realized that I may have spoken too soon. "Nothing. Why are you calling?"

"Oh no, that sounds too juicy to pass up. What trouble did you guys get into now?"

"We didn't get into any trouble."

"You two are always in trouble."

"Why are you calling?"

"Maybe I just like to hear the sound of your voice in the morning."

I scoffed.

"Whatever it is you're keeping from me, you know I'm going to find out."

"Who's your source?"

"Wouldn't you like to know."

"I'd like to know why you're calling."

She sighed. "Fine. You're no fun. I'd usually harass you a little more, but this is important."

"I'm listening."

34

"After I ran my story, I got a call from a girl who said she was sexually assaulted by Professor Matthews," Paris said.

She had my full attention. "Did she report it?"

"Well, here's the thing. She can't prove it was Professor Matthews."

"Tell me what happened," I said.

"She was a graduate student. Said Matthews made several inappropriate advances, which she declined. It wasn't long after that when she was attacked by a masked man in the parking lot of her apartment complex. He put a knife to her throat and forced her to comply."

"So, she never saw his face."

"Correct."

"What made her think it was Professor Matthews?"

She said he had the same build, and she recognized his eyes and his cologne. To this day, she says it still makes her sick anytime she smells it in a department store or if someone's wearing it."

"What type of cologne?"

"*Seduction Pour Homme*, by D'Ambrosio."

"Did she report the incident?"

"She didn't. She said that the assailant threatened to kill her if she went to the police. He knew where she lived. She said he tried to disguise his voice, but she was certain it was Matthews."

"So, there's no record of this?"

"No."

"When did this happen?"

"Last year."

"What's the girl's name?"

"You know that thing about me and my sources. Unless I can get her to agree to go public, I have to respect her privacy wishes."

"With no physical evidence, and after so much time has passed, this is a difficult one to pursue."

"She is well aware of that, and that's another reason why she's staying anonymous."

"So why did she call you?"

"Because she's convinced the Coed Killer is Matthews, and she doesn't want anyone else to suffer the same fate."

"Keep working that angle with her. She could save somebody else's life."

"I'll see what I can do. But like you said, it's a tough sell at this point. Matthews will deny it, and she'll get dragged through the mud."

I groaned. "Keep me posted."

"I will."

I thanked her and ended the call.

JD emerged from his stateroom, looking wrecked. His face was battered and bruised, as was mine. He staggered into the galley and poured a cup of coffee. We dished up and ate at the dining nook.

Isabella called. "I checked the phone records of the girl who allegedly overdosed on sleeping pills, Keira Bell. This is a little interesting."

"Do tell."

"The night of her death, she had exchanged a few calls with a burner phone. A lot of people use prepaid cellular phones for various reasons. Doesn't always imply nefarious activity, but I find it a little odd, especially given the circumstance. That burner phone last pinged the cell tower not far from Keira's apartment. It went off the grid afterward and has never resurfaced.

"I'd say that's suspicious."

"You know what's really interesting?"

"No, but you're about to tell me."

"Dayna Trammell called that burner phone just days before."

I lifted a surprised brow. "Now, that definitely warrants further investigation."

"Have you been to Keira's apartment complex? Talked to the neighbors?" Isabella asked. "Maybe somebody saw something."

"I think that's first on our agenda today."

After breakfast, we got a nice treat. Jack's phone rang, and his eyes lit up. A filtered voice crackled through the speaker.

Jack replied, "Yeah, now is a great time."

"Great. I'll be right over," the caller said.

JD ended the call, and a mischievous grin curled his lips.

"Who was that?"

"Zach. He's delivering our new boat."

I lifted a surprised brow. "You bought a boat?"

"I saw it online. Had to have it. We needed a replacement for the wake boat."

"How much?"

"Don't ask."

Zach Forrester & Associates was a luxury broker on the island. Zach had an angle on everything. His inventory was top notch, and his customer service was second to none. We'd bought the *Avventura* from him.

Zach arrived 15 minutes later in a stunning 25' *Yamazuki XP355*. It had a white hull with neon green trim and a Bimini top. 4600 lbs, a beam of 8' 7" and a draft of 19". It seated 12 and was fully loaded—hand-stitched upholstery, integrated swim platform, dining table, stainless steel reboarding ladder, integrated drink holders, touchscreens, push-button start, throttle by wire, and a pumping stereo system. It was the perfect little party boat. Twin 1.8 liter mega vortex high output engines, corrosion-resistant driveline, 75 gallon fuel capacity.

It was a beauty.

Zach pulled into an empty slip and tossed us the lines. We tied off, and Zach killed the engine. He climbed to the dock and handed Jack the keys. "Just a little paperwork, and she's all yours."

Jack beamed, and we both marveled at the new boat. It was a worthy replacement. I could already envision bikini-clad beauties lounging on the foredeck.

We did the transaction, and Forrester caught a cab back to his office. JD was already plotting our first adventure on the new boat. But first, there was work to do.

We drove up to Pineapple Bay and found the *Coral Bay* apartments. The community was a series of pastel-colored two-story walkups with wood siding and pitched roofs. Each unit had its own balcony. A concrete walkway snaked between the buildings. The grounds were landscaped with green grass, tall palms, and other foliage. It was a nice place. The complex was centered around an L-shaped swimming pool with lounge chairs and patio tables with umbrellas. It wasn't a gated community, and parking surrounded the units.

We pulled into the lot and drove around to the back to find apartment #201-C. It was painted pastel pink.

Keira's unit had long since been turned over, but I hoped to talk to one of the neighbors.

We walked up the steps to the shared veranda and banged on the door to unit 101, which was directly below Keira's old unit. The building was on pylons about 2 1/2 feet off the ground to accommodate any flooding.

Nobody answered at #101. We banged on the door to #102, and still no reply. We climbed the switchback staircase to the second floor and banged on door #202.

"Who is it?" a woman asked through the door.

I flashed my badge to the peephole. "Deputy Wild with Coconut County. I'd like to ask you some questions about Keira Bell. Were you living here at the time of her death?"

A cute brunette pulled open the door and surveyed us curiously. She had smooth tanned skin, blue eyes, and a light dusting of freckles. She was an all-natural beauty. No makeup. She wore a tank top and shorts and had slim, toned legs.

"Yeah, I've been living here for almost two years. Keira was a sweetheart. It's really terrible what happened. I didn't even know she was depressed."

"She may not have been," I said.

The woman's face crinkled.

"This is my partner Jack Donovan."

"I'm Penelope Jackson," She said. "I heard that she OD'd."

"Were you home the night Keira died?"

"Yeah, I think. I mean, they didn't find her body until like two days later. I guess her family was worried about her and contacted the apartment manager, Betty. She did a welfare check."

I said, "Her friend, Andrea, told us that Keira had just met a new guy."

Penelope's face tensed as she thought, and she bit her bottom lip. "Let me see, they found her on Tuesday. I think she OD'd some time Sunday night if I'm not mistaken."

"That's correct."

"Bear with me. This was several months ago." She searched her memory. "You know, I did see a guy come by Sunday night. He had roses and a bottle of wine, and she let him in." She paused. "I don't know how long he stayed. I left shortly after that and ended up spending the night with my boyfriend at the time."

"Do you remember what the guy looked like?"

"Yeah, he was good-looking. Older. Kind of mysterious."

"Can you describe him?"

She pondered the description for a moment. "He was tall. 6', 6'1" maybe. Dark blonde hair, almost brown. His hairline was kinda high, but it didn't take away from his features. Rugged face. Good body. He was a real man."

"When you say older, how old?"

She shrugged. "I'm not really good with that sort of thing. Mid 40s, maybe."

"You recall hearing his name?"

Penelope shook her head.

"What time did you leave your apartment?"

"8:30 or 9 PM. My boyfriend picked me up. We went out to dinner, went to a few bars, then back to his place."

"You think you could give a description to a sketch artist?"

"Sure," she said. "I don't see why not. Like I said, this was a few months ago, so the details are kind of fuzzy. I just saw the guy once."

"That was the only time he visited?"

"I don't know if that was the only time, but it was the only time I saw him."

"Thanks, this has been helpful. I'll have a sketch artist from the department contact you. Can I get your information?"

"Sure."

I gave her my phone number, and she texted me her information.

"If you can think of anything else that might be helpful, please let us know."

"Do you think that guy had something to do with her death?"

"That's what her best friend seems to think."

Penelope cringed. "That's terrible. Who would want to kill Keira?"

"That's what we're trying to find out. Did you know her well?"

She shook her head, and her hair swayed from side to side. "Not really. We'd say hello in passing. She was always sweet. She invited me over for wine one night."

"When was that?"

"Not long after she first moved in. We always planned to hang out sometime. But you know how life is, you get busy doing your own thing, and you forget to coordinate, then the moment passes you by."

I thanked her again, and we headed back down the steps to the parking lot. We hopped in the Porsche, pulled around to the front of the building, and found the manager's office to see if she had any additional insight.

35

"Are you thinking what I'm thinking?" JD asked.

"I'm thinking there might be something to Andrea's story. Keira's new boyfriend comes over with a bottle of wine, spikes her drink with sleeping pills, then slips out after she's gone."

"It's sounding more and more plausible."

We stopped into the office and spoke with Betty, the property manager. She expressed her condolences over the loss of Keira. "I really liked her. She was a good tenant. She paid her rent on time."

"Did she ever talk to you about her new boyfriend?"

"We really didn't talk much. Just occasionally here and there. I still have nightmares about finding her. There was absolutely no color in her face. Her lips were blue, and her skin was pale as could be. She was just in her bed, looking almost peaceful."

"Did you notice anything unusual at the time?"

"Aside from the fact that she was dead?"

"Anything missing?"

"I wouldn't know if anything was missing or not. There was an empty jar of acetaminophen by the bed, along with an empty bottle of nonprescription sleeping pills. It's my understanding the combination causes liver toxicity. But what do I know?" She paused, and her eyes surveyed us. "Judging by the questions you're asking, you think something funny is going on."

"There could very well be," I said.

I gave her my card and told her to call me if she could think of anything else.

We headed back to Coconut Key, and by the time we arrived, Jack was ready for lunch. We got a quick bite to eat at *Diver Down,* then headed over to *Sandpiper Point* to confront Dayna. We figured she wouldn't talk, but her reaction would be enough. I had asked Isabella to monitor her communications.

We boarded the *Sea Eye Hey* and shuffled along the side deck to the foredeck, where we found her lounging on the sun pad. The brilliant sun glistened on her oiled legs. Dayna looked good in a royal blue bikini, her blue eyes covered by oversized sunglasses. A wide-brimmed straw hat shaded her pretty face. Music filtered through speakers. She didn't notice us at first. I cleared my throat, and she sat up on her elbows. Even through the dark sunglasses, I could tell she glared at us with disdain.

Langston wasn't around.

"What are you doing here? This is private property."

"We just have some follow-up questions for you."

"I told you, if you have any questions, talk to my attorney. If you have something, then arrest me. If not, leave."

"Don't worry. We're on our way out. But I find it interesting that you were calling the guy that Keira was dating at the time of her death."

Dayna tried to hide a stunned expression, not doing a very good job of it. "I'm not sure where you're getting your information from, Deputy, but—"

I cut her off. "Save it. You're just gonna dig yourself a deeper hole. You know what I think? I think Langley had a problem. Which means *you* had a problem. I've only known you for a brief time, but you seem like a take-charge kind of woman. You know what you want, and you go after it. The allegations against Langley were not in your plan. And quite frankly, they were a little embarrassing for you."

She said nothing.

"I think you made a phone call to someone who could make Langston's legal problems go away."

She swallowed hard.

"That makes you an accessory to murder."

"That's ridiculous. Keira OD'd. Everyone knows it."

"I think the guy you hired poisoned her. He showed up at her apartment with a bottle of wine and the promise of a good time."

Dayna's whole body tensed, and her tanned face started to look a little peaked. "I want you to leave now."

"No problem. We're on our way out." We left the foredeck, and before I disappeared around the bulkhead, I called back over my shoulder. "We'll be in touch."

We made our way aft, crossed the gangway to the dock, and walked toward the parking lot.

"I think you rattled her cage a little."

I grinned. "Let's see how frazzled she gets."

36

"Dayna just called a burner phone," Isabella said. "Sounded pretty frantic. She said, '*Two cops just came by. They know. How do they know?*' Whoever she called didn't respond. They just hung up."

"You get a location on the burner?" I asked.

"I did. 1502 Laughing Gull Lane."

"Let me know if she makes any other phone calls."

"You got it," Isabella said before ending the call.

We headed back to the station and swapped the Porsche out with the surveillance van. The vinyl wrap made it look like an air conditioning repair company. We recruited one of the IT guys, Crenshaw, for the mission. The three of us hustled across the island to Laughing Gull. We parked a few houses down at the curb across the street.

The house wasn't much to look at from the outside. A 6-foot tall wooden fence, stained rust-colored, surrounded the property. There were tall palms in the yard that extended above the one-story roof. The house was white stucco. Probably a two-bedroom. There was a white pickup truck parked at the curb. A gravel drive was secured by a wooden gate. There was a green trash bin at the end of the driveway.

It was a modest neighborhood—nothing too flashy.

Crenshaw was well-versed in all the hacker techniques. He had a backpack full of goodies and gadgets, wireless network sniffers, and special applications that could probe for vulnerabilities in networks. The average home network is surprisingly unsecure.

We set up shop, and Crenshaw manned the control terminal. There were two large flatscreen displays that provided multiple views from the ultra-high-def cameras positioned around the van. It was state-of-the-art stuff. The kind of cameras that could read a license plate from a mile away easily.

We focused in on the residence.

Crenshaw pulled his laptop from his backpack, flipped open the screen, and launched an application. He started probing the networks, and based on signal strength, he was able to get an idea of which network belonged to our suspect. His fingers clacked the keys, and the kid worked his magic. After a few minutes of futzing around, he gave us a grim look.

"This guy knows what he's doing. I can't find any vulnerabilities in his system. No smart devices, nothing to hack. If you want to get eyes or ears inside that place, you'll have to do it the old-fashioned way."

I figured if Dayna had just called him in a panic, he'd have his guard up. One of us could dress up as a utility worker with a neon vest and hardhat and go knocking on neighborhood doors asking about power fluctuations or other such nonsense. But a tactic like that might tip this guy off.

Isabella told me that the house was rented in the name of a company that was owned by another offshore company, obscuring the true ownership. It was a red flag that tipped me off right away. Normal people don't go to that kind of trouble to hide ownership.

I figured this was the kind of guy who'd change his phone on a regular basis and might bug out at the first sign of trouble. Something told me this was a hitman for hire, a professional. He was used to dealing with high-end clients that paid top dollar to get the job done without questions. There were a lot easier ways to kill Keira Bell than to seduce her and slip enough sleeping pills and acetaminophen in her drink to cause organ failure. But it was clean and had gone unnoticed for months. That was the type of operator we were dealing with. And he was smart enough not to respond to Dayna when she called on an unencrypted channel. I figured that probably didn't sit well with him. It wouldn't sit well with me if I were a hitman.

We sat around for half an hour, contemplating our next move.

Isabella had told me that the burner phone Dayna called had gone off the grid, but the last data she had for it placed it in the house on Laughing Gull. It was my guess that whoever was in possession of the phone would get rid of it soon and never use it again. It was foolish to use a burner phone from your own location. But, everybody slips up. You get lazy. Complacent. Cocky. Especially when you think no one is watching.

Another 20 minutes went by, then a man emerged from the pedestrian gate in front of the house. He walked around and climbed into the driver's seat of the pickup truck.

Crenshaw zoomed in with the ultra-high-definition camera and got a good look at his face.

He matched the description Penelope had given me.

I told Crenshaw to export a few screen grabs and send them to my phone.

I texted the images to Isabella as the man cranked up the pickup truck and pulled away from the curb.

I started up the van, and we followed, hanging back a safe distance.

37

"Ian Goddard," Isabella said when she called back. "He's a known pro. A fixer. Corporate type. Lotta high-end clients."

"Figures."

"His record is clean. And I mean spotless. It's been scrubbed. I'm pretty sure he's got friends in high places."

"Not high enough," I said.

"I'm sure he's paid a lot of money to grease the right palms. The guy's dangerous. Be careful."

"Always."

I ended the call and texted a picture of Ian to Penelope Jackson. "Is that the guy?"

She replied a few minutes later. "That's him!"

"You're sure?

"Positive."

We followed him to the Mega Mart. It was a big box retailer with groceries, electronics, clothing, entertainment, bicycles, lawn furniture, and anything else you could imagine. He put on a hat and sunglasses and hopped out of the truck. Ian walked toward the entrance. He tossed the burner phone in the trash before he stepped inside. I figured he was picking up another prepaid phone.

If you were really paranoid, you wouldn't even buy a prepaid phone yourself, though a disguise would help. You get a *"cut out"* as they call it in the industry—someone you found on the street to stand in for you. It could be kind of risky, giving a homeless guy a couple hundred bucks to walk in and buy a prepaid phone loaded up. But that was the surest way to get a device that could never be connected to you. Each phone has a unique identifier and can be tracked to the point of purchase. Most stores have surveillance video, and even if you pay in cash, it may be possible to discover your identity through facial recognition. Though Ian's disguise would make it more difficult.

I decided to roll the dice and see if I could rattle his nerves. I hopped out of the van and hustled to the main exit of the store and waited. Ian was inside for about 15 minutes. He stepped out with a plastic bag in hand containing a box that looked like a prepaid cell phone.

He walked right past me.

"Ian Goddard?" I asked, flashing my badge.

He hesitated for a moment, then kept walking.

I followed along. "We know Dayna hired you to take care of Keira Bell. I've got a witness that can put you at Keira's apartment the night of her death. It's only a matter of time before this all comes together. I'm guessing she hired you to take out Fawn DiCarlo, too. But I'm still piecing it together."

Ian said nothing. He didn't even look in my direction. He walked to the truck, clicked the key fob, and the lights flashed. As he climbed inside, I said, "Dayna is going to crack. You know that. She's not a cool customer like you are."

He pulled the door shut, cranked up the engine, and pulled out of the space. I stepped away from the vehicle. I didn't think he'd run me over in broad daylight, but he probably wanted to.

I jogged back to the surveillance van, hopped inside, and said, "Let the games begin, gentlemen."

38

W e drove the van back to the station and dropped Crenshaw off. Isabella texted me and said that Dayna was on the move. She was tracking her phone and would give me updates. She sent a text a few minutes later that Dayna was at the Highland Village Mall. It was an upscale, open-air shopping center filled with designer boutiques. I figured the stress had gotten to Dayna, and she needed a little *retail therapy*.

We hopped into the Porsche and headed to the mall. The parking lot was filled with BMWs, Mercedes, Landrovers, and other high-end cars. Ladies pranced around the courtyard carrying designer bags. The smell of fast food wafted from the food court, and chill music pumped through speakers. A cool breeze flowed between the storefronts, and brilliant rays of sunshine beat down. There were trees and plants and benches where you could hang out and people watch. There was always plenty of eye candy at Highland Village. The island's uber wealthy thought nothing of dropping five figures on a spree, sometimes six.

Isabella told us we could find Dayna at *Charmante Couture*. They were known for their handmade bespoke dresses tailored to your exact specifications. We pushed inside and found Dayna browsing the racks. Her eyes flicked to us as we entered.

The sales associate instantly pounced. "Good afternoon, gentlemen. How can I help you?"

I pointed to Dayna.

The sales clerk smiled and backed away.

A look of repulsion twisted on Dayna's face.

"I told you, I'm not speaking with you." She called the sales clerk. "These two men are harassing me."

The sales clerk's face went long. "Gentlemen, you'll have to leave right now before I call security," she said, trying to sound intimidating.

I flashed my badge. "That won't be necessary."

Her wide eyes flicked from me to Dayna, then back again. She looked utterly perplexed.

I told Dayna that she didn't need to speak with us. We would do all the talking. "I just had an interesting conversation with Ian Goddard."

Her face grew tight, and she swallowed hard.

"He's not too happy with you."

Dayna's nervous eyes flicked to the sales clerk. The clerk took the opportunity to bow out and disappear into the back. She wanted no part of this.

"I don't know anyone by that name," Dayna said.

"Really? Is that why you just called him?"

"I don't know what you're talking about."

"Here's the way I see it. Ian is a professional. He's used to pressure. You're not. He knows that. Now that this thing is out in the open, you're a liability. You connect him to Keira Bell and Fawn DiCarlo."

She held her body rigid but that didn't stop the tremors.

"This is your opportunity to come clean. Rollover on everyone involved, and maybe you'll get a reduced sentence. The way it stands right now. I'd watch your back."

Fear bathed her eyes, and she had no sunglasses to hide behind.

"Think about it."

I turned around and walked out of the store with JD. I'd made my point.

39

The show was about to begin.

We ambled through the open-air mall, taking in the sights—long legs with designer heels and perfectly manicured fingers grasping couture shopping bags. We stopped in a department store and made our way to the cologne counter. An older woman with dyed black hair gave me a sample of *Seduction Pour Homme*.

I opened the vial and sniffed the expensive fragrance. It was distinctly sweet and sharp.

"It's my favorite scent," the clerk said, batting her false eyelashes. "I could smell it all day."

"It's interesting."

JD sniffed it, and his nose crinkled.

"All the ladies love it," the clerk said. "Not that you'd need any help in that department."

I smirked appreciatively.

"You ready to take a bottle with you?"

"Not at this time, thank you."

She frowned. "Come see me if you change your mind."

We left and headed toward the parking lot.

I had no doubt in my mind that Dayna wasn't going to handle the situation well. She was the type that was always in control, and this situation was spiraling. It was only a matter of time.

Isabella told me that Dayna's next call was to Langston. By the time we reached the Porsche, Isabella had sent me an .mp3 of the call. It wasn't exactly legal and wouldn't be admissible, unfortunately.

Any connected device can be hacked, some easier than others. Most people sacrifice privacy for convenience and aren't willing to go through the necessary lengths to protect it. She should have called Langston using an end-to-end encrypted app.

I pressed play, and we listened to the call.

"They followed me to the fucking mall," Dayna screeched.

"Calm down," Langston replied. It was the wrong thing to say.

"Don't tell me to calm down!" she hissed.

From the background noise, I could tell she had left the boutique and was walking through the courtyard.

"They know everything. They know about Keira. They know about Fawn."

"Don't be so stupid. They don't know anything."

"Don't call me stupid."

Langston sighed. "They don't know. They *suspect*. If they *knew* and could prove it, you'd be in handcuffs right now."

"And so would you. We are all in this together. Don't you forget that."

"Have you talked to Ian?"

"He's pissed. He finally called me back from another phone on an encrypted app. He's ultra paranoid. It's not like they can listen to our calls, can they? I mean, they need a warrant for that kind of stuff, right?"

"They need probable cause, and they don't have it. Just relax. They're trying to rattle you, and it's clearly working."

"How can you be so calm?"

"Because they've got nothing. You paid the guy in crypto. They can't track that. And if you don't say anything to them, they will continue to have nothing."

"Ian got pissed because I called him. They've already talked to him."

Langston hesitated a moment. "How do they know about Ian?"

"I don't know. But they know. That's what I'm telling you. Are you starting to get it now? This is serious."

He stammered, "What did Ian say?"

"To keep our mouths shut and to never contact him again."

"Like never?"

"That's what he said."

"What if we need his services again?"

"We'll find someone else if the need arises. I'm not doing business with him again."

"Why not?"

"That fucker didn't take care of Fawn."

"What do you mean?"

"I mean, I paid him $50,000 for nothing. I told him I want my money back."

"What did he say?"

"No refunds."

"If he didn't kill Fawn, who did?"

"I don't know. But I shouldn't have to pay for it."

"You didn't pay for anything," Langston snarked. "It's daddy's money."

"Shut up. Where does your money come from!?"

Langston said nothing.

After a long moment of silence, Dayna asked, "What are we going to do?"

"Ian's a rock. He's not going to talk. He knows better. If we split town, we'll look guilty."

"Yeah, but I'm not going down for this. We should get out now while we can. We can take a long vacation in a country without an extradition treaty and let this whole thing die down."

Langston was silent again for a moment. "Okay. Where do you want to go?"

"I don't know. Someplace tropical with good nightlife."

"Those are your only two requirements?"

"Well, it can't be a shit hole. I want fast Internet, a day spa, and access to organic food."

Langston groaned. "We're going on the run, Dayna. This isn't a vacation."

"Doesn't mean we have to make sacrifices."

Langston sighed. "I'll start looking around for places. We probably shouldn't talk on the phone like this anymore either."

"I thought you said they couldn't listen to our calls."

"They can't, but..." He paused. "We'll talk more when I see you."

The call ended, and I exchanged a curious glance with JD. He asked, "If Ian didn't kill Fawn, who did?"

I shrugged.

"We need to get something solid on them before they skip town," Jack said.

That would be a tall order. Langston was right. We didn't have probable cause to subpoena phone records. We didn't have anything legitimate to connect Dayna Trammell with Ian Goddard. We had nothing. I called Denise and asked her to contact the phone company and request the data anyway, but without a warrant, they wouldn't comply.

I got a call from Paris Delaney as we drove back to *Diver Down*. "My source has agreed to go public. Say *'Thank you, Paris.'*"

"Thank you, Paris."

"I'm airing the interview tonight. Should be explosive."

"Is she willing to make a sworn affidavit and testify in court?"

"Slow your roll, Cowboy. One thing at a time. I got her to agree to the interview."

"I'd like to talk to her."

"Come down to the studio and talk to her after I do my segment. I don't want you spooking her beforehand."

"What time are you filming?"

"She should be here in half an hour. Fingers crossed."

"We're on our way."

JD changed course, and we headed for the studio.

W e joined Paris on the soundstage. The nightly news desks were the focal piece of the room. Behind them, a seamless green screen for compositing in the background.

The desks were empty now, and so was the sound stage. A lighting grid hung overhead, and the walls were painted black and lined with sound-dampening material.

The crew for this interview was kept to a minimum—just Paris, two cameramen, and a sound guy. To the side of the main news set, they had set up a scene for the interview. Lights in softboxes cast a flattering glow on both Paris and her subject as they sat across from each other. Behind them, a gray background painted with a swath of colored light and a fake plant. It would all be blurred out. Lit with Rembrandt style Portrait Lighting, it created an intimate mood fitting for the grim subject matter.

We stood near the main camera as Paris began the interview. Mia Crawford recounted her harrowing tale in excruciating detail. More than once, she broke down into sobs as the old wounds were re-opened. The details were exactly as Paris described to me previously. Hearing it straight from Mia's mouth made it all the more heart-wrenching.

"Your attacker was never apprehended, correct?" Paris stated.

Mia nodded. "That's correct."

"But you believe you know who's responsible."

"Yes," Mia said, wiping her teary eyes.

"Can you tell us the name of this person?"

Mia paused for a moment, her lip quivering, her body trembling. Her eyes flicked away for a moment, and torment tensed her face. She bit her bottom lip.

Finally, "Professor Evan Matthews."

She exhaled, and it was like a weight was lifted from her. She broke down into sobs, and Paris gave her a moment to compose herself.

"Why do you believe he's the man that attacked you?"

She recounted the details and her experience of unwanted advances as a student of Professor Matthews.

"And why are you choosing to come forward now?"

"Because I don't want anyone else to go through what I endured."

"Deputies from the Coconut County Sheriff's Department are here to speak with you. Thank you for your bravery. I know how difficult this is for you."

Paris wrapped up the interview and chatted with Mia off-camera for a few moments. Paris then waved us over. Now that the cat was out of the bag, Mia agreed to make a sworn affidavit.

Even with her statement, there was nothing concrete against Matthews. There was no physical evidence tying him to the crime. The alleged sexual misconduct was just that. Alleged. He made advances, she declined. He used his position of authority in an attempt to coerce her, but it wouldn't stand up.

Surprisingly, Judge Echols gave us a warrant. We found Matthews on campus in an auditorium teaching a molecular biology course. He gave us a curious look as we entered the classroom and descended the steps to the podium. I presented the warrant, and a look of utter disbelief washed over his face.

Jaws dropped. The class was silent as JD slapped the metal cuffs around his wrists.

Matthews was apoplectic. In a blustery tone, he shouted, "This is preposterous. I will have both of your badges for this."

I rolled my eyes.

JD took him by the arm and escorted him out of the classroom.

The students almost wanted to burst into cheers, but they restrained themselves, probably for fear of reprisal. The stern professor was loathed on campus.

We marched him across the quad, a long walk of shame, and handed him over to Mendoza and Robinson. They stuffed him into the back of the patrol car and took him down to the station.

We followed and filled out after-action reports, then took a crack at him in the interrogation room.

Matthews was flustered. His skin was slick, and his cheeks red. The veins in his temples pulsed. The distinct smell of Seduction Pour Homme by D'Ambrosio lingered in the air.

"Tell me about Mia Crawford," I said.

In a slow and deliberate tone, he replied, "I want to speak with an attorney."

That was the end of the interview.

I didn't expect him to talk. He would spend the night in jail, get arraigned in the morning, and the DA would refuse to take the case based on lack of evidence.

I pushed away from the table, stood up, and marched out of the room. It didn't take long for Juliana Morgan to call to give me an earful.

"What have you done?"

"Word travels fast, doesn't it?" I said.

"You're destroying a man's life and reputation. What grounds do you have to arrest Evan?"

"I suggest you watch Paris Delaney's report at 9 PM and at 11 PM."

She clenched her jaw and growled. "That woman is a sensationalist ambulance chaser. She looks for drama where none exists."

"Listen to Mia Crawford's story, and let me know if you still feel the same way about your beloved professor. I'm sorry, but your boyfriend is going down, sooner or later."

"He is not my boyfriend. He's a respected colleague and a—"

"I know, a wonderful educator. He's also a murderer and a rapist. I hope you see that before it's too late."

I ended the call.

JD looked at his watch. "I think it's about time for a celebratory cocktail."

I wasn't going to argue, but it wasn't time to celebrate just yet.

41

"You're sure she's not dating that sicko?" JD asked with a drink in hand.

We'd stopped in for the happy hour special at *Wetsuit*. The drinks had been served, and the waitress clanked down a seafood platter for an appetizer—fried shrimp, scampi shrimp, scallops, crab balls, calamari, and lobster.

"If you need anything else, let me know," she said with a smile before darting away.

"I'm not sure of anything," I said. "But Juliana's mentioned a few times now that she's not seeing Evan romantically. Though, I don't think you have a shot. In case you haven't noticed, we're not on her list of favorite people."

"She just hasn't gotten to know us yet," JD said, ever the optimist. He sipped his whiskey and stuffed a crab ball in his mouth. Before he finished chewing, he asked, "What are we gonna do about Dayna and her boyfriend?"

"Isabella's monitoring their comms and movements. If they try to leave the country, there's not much we can do to stop them."

We were halfway through the seafood platter when my phone buzzed with a call from the peeper, CJ Mackey. I swiped the screen and held the phone to my ear.

"Deputy Wild?" he asked in a panicked breath.

"What can I do for you?"

"I need your help."

"Oh, now you need my help?"

"These men are after me."

"What men?"

"The men that were in Fawn DiCarlo's apartment."

"So, now you're admitting to peeping on your neighbor?"

"Are you going to help me or not?"

"Where are you right now?"

"Is this line secure?"

"Yes, it is." We weren't talking on an encrypted call, but I was pretty sure the people that were after CJ Mackey weren't listening to my phone.

"I'm at Key Bean. I'm in the back in a booth. I don't think they followed me."

"Stay there. We'll be right over. Don't go anywhere. Don't call anyone else."

"Got it."

I ended the call and filled JD in. He stuffed as many appetizers in his mouth as would fit, then washed it all down with the last swig of whiskey. He flagged the waitress down, handed her a wad of cash, and we darted out of the bar.

My guess was that CJ Mackey had seen something he wasn't supposed to see.

We hustled down the sidewalk. Key Bean wasn't far away, but Jack's belly cramped as we jogged down the sidewalk to the eclectic coffee shop.

The smell of fresh brew filled the air as we stepped inside. The gentle murmur of conversation drifted about, mixed with the sound of an espresso machine. The barista called out a name. "Susan! Susan, your order is ready."

Light jazz filtered through speakers. My eyes surveyed the coffee shop, and I caught sight of CJ in the back booth, leaning around the seatback with wide eyes. He motioned us toward him.

I surveyed the area for threats. It seemed clear, but I kept my head on a swivel, like always.

We slid into the bench seat across the table from him.

"Tell me exactly what's going on," I demanded. "No bullshit this time."

42

"**A**re you sure you weren't followed?" CJ asked.

"We weren't followed," I said, trying not to sound too annoyed.

"These two guys showed up at the apartment."

"The same guys as before?"

He hesitated and stared into my eyes. "I'm not getting in trouble, am I?"

"Tell me everything."

He took a deep breath, then exhaled. "Okay, yeah, I may have observed my neighbor on a few occasions."

I arched a knowing eyebrow at him.

"Okay, maybe more than a few occasions."

"How often?"

He shrugged. "I mean, that girl was hot. Who could blame me? Every day she would come home and peel off her clothes with the blinds open. She didn't care who was watching. It's like she wanted me to look."

I scolded him with my eyes.

"Then I figured out who she was and what she did. Like clockwork, she'd get on the computer and put on a little show." His eyes rounded. "Let me tell you, that was pure entertainment. I got to see it all for free."

"Tell me about the guys," I said.

"I didn't say anything before because, you know... I didn't want to look like some kinda creep. Then I thought, maybe I might have to testify. All these questions would come up, and everyone would find out—"

"Just get to the point."

"So, I'm pretty sure it was the night that Fawn disappeared. Two guys entered her apartment. They had a key. They came in and tore through the place. And they weren't too gentle about it. They were tossing seat cushions around, looking in pillowcases, they searched under the mattress, they looked in all the kitchen cabinets, the bathroom, every-where. In the closet they found a kilo of coke. At least, I think it was coke. Could have been heroin, could have been flower or sugar for all I know. But it was wrapped up and packaged like you see on those drug shows." He raised his hands innocently. "I don't do coke, so I don't know what it looks like."

"Sure," I said, not inclined to believe his denial.

His eyes narrowed at me. "Anyway, the guys left the apart-ment, and that was that. Flash forward to today, and they came back. They did the little search party routine again, looking through the cushions, checking all the places they missed. Pulling open drawers, going through the entire apartment again. I happened to notice the lights were on and aimed my telescope in that direction and watched. That's when one of the guys saw me, just like you did. He did the same damn thing. He told his buddy he was gonna find me and marched across the street. He didn't have a pleasant look on his face, let me tell you. These were guys you don't want to mess with. Big, muscular, mean-looking. One of them was bald, the other one had short dark hair. Anyway, it didn't take a rocket scientist to figure out these guys were going to be banging on my door in a couple seconds. So I got the hell out of Dodge. I took the stairwell down to the street, took off on foot, and called you when I got here."

The minute he described the guys, I knew who he was talking about. It had to be Archer and Cole.

"You think you could identify these guys from a photo?"

"Yeah, I got a real good look at them."

I showed CJ their DMV photos on my phone.

"Yeah, those are the guys."

"You sure about this?"

"I'm positive." His eyes flicked between the two of us. "It's pretty clear Fawn had something they wanted besides the coke, and I don't think they found it." He leaned in and spoke in a hushed tone. "And you know what I think? I think they killed her for it."

"Did you figure that out all by yourself?" I asked with more than a hint of sarcasm.

CJ's face crinkled. "Hey, I'm helping you guys out. You guys would be running around chasing your tail without me."

"And you have no one to protect you without us," I said.

He leaned back and tucked his chin with a frown.

"Are you willing to testify to what you have seen?"

"You're going to keep me safe, right? I mean, I can't go back to my apartment now. They know I know what they look like." He frowned. "I know all you got on them right now is breaking and entering, right? You still have no evidence to connect them to Fawn's murder. If you arrest them, they're going to get out in a day. They will come after me."

"We can put you in a safe location for the time being."

"What's a safe location?"

"The Seven Seas."

He lifted an intrigued eyebrow. "Really? All expenses paid?"

"It's not a vacation."

"I mean, you'll cover my meals and bar tab, right?"

"Just don't go crazy with the minibar, and I'm sure the county will cover it."

43

W e escorted CJ down the sidewalk, keeping a watchful eye. I opened the passenger door to the Porsche, pulled the seat forward, and let him climb in the back. It was comical, to say the least. He was too big to fit. I pulled the seat as far forward as I could go, but it was a tight squeeze.

We took him back to the station, and he gave a statement. Then we got him set up with a suite at the *Seven Seas*. I made him shut off his cell phone before the drive over.

We put him on the second floor, and I told him, "Don't contact anyone. And I mean *anyone*. You understand?"

CJ nodded.

"We're not posting a guard. Keep your phone off, and don't use it for anything. Don't surf the web, don't watch porn."

He frowned at me.

"If you need to call someone, and that someone would be *me*, use the landline. In fact, give me your cell phone."

His face crinkled.

"I'm not giving you my cell phone."

I extended my palm. "Hand it over. I've lost way too many witnesses that have made stupid mistakes." His eyes rounded, and a worried look tensed his face. "You've lost witnesses?"

"Witnesses who did dumb stuff like call a friend or relative while they were in hiding."

He looked at me with eyes that needed reassurance.

"Don't do anything stupid, and you'll be just fine. Stay in your room, order room service."

"For how long?"

"For as long as it takes," I said slowly, enunciating clearly.

I motioned for the phone again.

"It's off. I promise it will stay that way."

I gave him a stern gaze and reluctantly let him keep it. "We'll be in touch."

He closed the door, latched the deadbolt, and attached the security chain. We ambled down the hallway and took the elevator to the lobby. It was busy with people doing late check-ins and guests milling about. The hotel bar always had a good crowd, and tonight was no exception.

JD caught sight of a leggy blonde and nudged me with his elbow. He veered off course with a sly grin on his face. I followed him into the bar, and he sauntered right up to the counter next to her and ordered two whiskeys. Her straight blonde hair dangled at her mid-back. She wore a tight cocktail dress that left little to the imagination, and her long, tanned legs shimmered with moisturizer.

"You know, drinking alone is the first sign of a problem," JD muttered over his shoulder.

"Excuse me?" she asked, mildly annoyed.

"Well, now that we're here, you're not really alone, are you? So, I guess you can finish your drink."

Her eyes narrowed at him, unimpressed. "I'm waiting for a friend."

"Is she cute?"

"All my friends are cute."

"Like, how cute? Like, *my dog's cute?* Or cute, like *hot*?"

"My friends are not dogs."

"Be honest, who's better looking. You or your friend."

She seemed both annoyed and intrigued by JD's line of interrogation. She arched a curious eyebrow. "My friend is absolutely gorgeous. Way out of your league."

JD smiled. "That's okay. I'll settle for you."

"Settle?"

"I'm willing to take one for the team and jump on a grenade so my buddy here can focus on your friend."

She was absolutely stunned. "A grenade?"

"I bet you could be explosive when someone lights your fuse."

"And I suppose you think you can light my fuse?"

"You're not really my type," JD said. She was totally his type. "But, if you have a good personality, that makes up for a lot."

"Does this little routine often work for you?"

"You'd be surprised," I said.

She gave me a curious look.

I extended my hand. "I'm Tyson, by the way. This is JD."

"I'd say it's nice to meet you, but the jury's out. I haven't decided yet."

"That's okay. JD can be an acquired taste."

He smiled.

"Are you two from out of town?"

"No. We're local."

"I see. Just prowling the hotel bars, looking for some tourist action?"

"Just having a drink after a long day at the office," I said.

"So you don't have a room here?" she asked, assessing the situation.

"I'm sure it wouldn't be too hard to get one."

Her eyes flicked between JD and me.

"Tell you what, the night is young. Why don't you grab a room and the three of us can have some fun."

I lifted a curious brow and exchanged a glance with JD.

"There are one too many sausages at that party," JD said. "What happened to your friend?"

"You can go one at a time if you like. Think of it as a two for one special."

I was beginning to get the picture. There were always working girls in the bar, especially during times of conventions and high seasonal traffic.

"How much?" I asked out of curiosity.

"You know what they say about price? If you have to ask..."

I dug into my pocket. "I'm gonna pull something out, and you tell me if it's enough."

I slipped out my shiny gold badge and discreetly displayed it.

Her sultry, enterprising gaze faded. She crinkled her upper lip. "Shit." A resigned sigh escaped her plump lips. "So, you gonna bust me, or are we gonna take it out in trade?"

44

"You know a girl named Fawn DiCarlo?" I asked. "She's in your line of work."

She shook her head. "You're probably not going to believe this, but I don't really do this that often. I just got in a bind and needed extra cash."

I didn't believe her.

"This is a dangerous line of work. Especially with random strangers that you haven't vetted."

She cringed. "I know."

"Do you have a manager?" I asked, phrasing it nicely.

"I don't."

"You're young and pretty. You are better than this."

Her face twisted with sadness. "I know. This isn't exactly how I saw my life going."

"I'm not going to bust you. Just find another line of work."

"Thank you. You guys are so sweet."

"Have you been busted before?"

She bit her bottom lip and shook her head. "Anytime this has happened before, they've always taken me up on my *trade* offer." She shrugged sheepishly.

I sighed and exchanged a glance with JD.

To my surprise, CJ Mackey walked into the bar, looking for trouble. His grin faded as soon as he saw us.

"What were my instructions?" I said.

CJ froze and swallowed hard, his eyes darting between JD and me, catching on the gorgeous blonde in between us. "You told me to stay in the room."

I excused myself from the blonde and stepped to CJ. "You need to go back to the room right now and don't come out."

"I just wanted a drink. Am I supposed to sit cooped up in that room 24/7?"

"If you don't want anybody to know you're here, that's exactly what you need to do."

He frowned.

"Turn around and go. Now!"

His face crinkled. "You guys are no fun."

He turned around and sulked out of the bar.

I rejoined JD and the blonde.

"Friend of yours?" she asked.

"Something like that. What's your name?"

She hesitated. "Ashley."

It was probably a fake name.

"Be careful, Ashley."

She nodded. "I'm done. No more. I'm going home right now."

I didn't believe that either.

My phone buzzed with a call from Isabella. "Dayna and Langston are on the move."

"We gotta roll," I said to JD.

Ashley wiggled her fingers at us as we hustled out of the bar. We pushed into the lot and ran to the Porsche while Isabella kept me updated. "They just left Sandpiper Point. They're heading northeast on Birchwood."

JD slid behind the wheel and cranked up the engine. He pulled out of the space and raced across the parking lot.

"Sit tight," Isabella said. "They're heading your way. Looks like they might be going to the airport."

We paused at the entrance to the lot. We watched cars crisscross the roadway.

A moment later, Isabella said, "They're coming up on your location."

We watched a midnight blue Mercedes SUV pass by. I caught a glimpse of Langston behind the wheel, but the tinted windows made it hard to see inside.

JD turned onto the highway right behind them.

"I'll let you take it from here," Isabella said.

"I appreciate you."

"I know."

We followed the SUV. If Dayna and Langston were skipping town, there wasn't much we could do to stop them. Perhaps one of the most frustrating things is knowing someone is guilty but not being able to prove it.

JD put a few car lengths between us. It was a good thing too.

The car exploded.

Bits of shrapnel and debris sprayed in all directions.

Metal twisted, and glass shattered.

An amber ball enveloped the vehicle, and black smoke roiled into the night sky.

The SUV rolled over from the blast, which originated underneath the car, and skidded off the road in a fiery heap.

The smell of gasoline, oil, and burning rubber filled the air —a toxic swirl.

Bits of blistering debris rained down.

JD pulled to the shoulder behind the flaming wreckage, and we hopped out. The heat coming off the blaze was intense and kept us at bay. The amber glow illuminated our faces.

The traffic crawled to a stop in both directions.

The blast originated under the driver's seat, killing Langston instantly. The vehicle lay on its side. Dayna was trapped in the blaze. If she had survived the initial blast, she wouldn't last long in the fire.

A passerby hopped out of his truck with a small fire extinguisher that was no match for the blaze.

Metal popped and pinged, and fire crackled.

I dialed 911, and within minutes, the Fire Department arrived and doused the vehicle. The air filled with a mix of steam and smoke as they brought the fire under control. The once midnight blue paint was now charred black and peeling. Wet ash and soot covered the smoldering SUV.

Red and white lights flickered, and emergency personnel swarmed the area—EMTs, paramedics, arson investigators, and the bomb squad. Brenda and her crew arrived. The charred bodies were removed, and investigators sifted through the rubble.

There were a million bits and pieces scattered about the road and shoulder. Somehow, we'd have to piece enough fragments together to get an idea of the materials used for the bomb. With any luck, we could trace them back to their point of purchase.

45

We found fragments of a battery, a pipe, and wiring. It was a pretty typical pipe bomb triggered by a disposable cell phone. A call or text could trip the relay. The external battery would provide the charge and detonate the device. With any luck, gunpowder residue on the pipe fragments could be analyzed and identified. There was no doubt in my mind that Ian Goddard was getting rid of loose ends that could tie him to the death of Keira Bell.

Now all I had to do was connect him with the bomb.

Then there was the matter of Fawn DiCarlo. I needed to link Simon Brennan's thugs to her abduction. With CJ's statement, I was pretty sure we could get a warrant for breaking and entering. But connecting Simon's thugs to anything else could prove difficult.

Paris Delaney had arrived, as had crews from several other stations. It was too juicy of an event to pass up.

"Deputy Wild, what can you tell us about the incident?" Paris asked, a boom microphone suddenly hovering over my head.

The lights from the camera squinted my eyes. "The vehicle exploded on the highway and burst into flames. Two occupants are deceased."

"Arson investigators and the bomb squad are on the scene. Was this a targeted attack?"

"We believe a pipe bomb was used."

"The car's registered to Langston Hughes," Paris said. The license plates were still visible. "Can you confirm that he is one of the deceased?"

"I can't speak any further about the incident at this time."

I stepped out of frame.

Paris spun around and faced the camera. "A devastating scene here in Coconut Key tonight, resulting in the tragic death of two youths, one of which may have been an heir to the immense fortune of Jordan Hughes. The passenger in the vehicle is still unknown. I'm Paris Delaney, and you heard it from me first."

The camera cut and Paris chased after me without the crew.

"You know who the passenger is?"

"I do, and you will find out in good time."

"It's Dayna Trammell, isn't it?"

"How do you know these things?"

"She's all over his social media feed. It doesn't take a genius to put two and two together. Do you know where they were going? Who targeted them? And why?"

"It's all speculation at this point."

She eyed me curiously. "What are you not telling me?"

I chuckled. "A lot."

"Now, now, Deputy. You know I can be a valuable asset. We're both on the same team."

"How is that?"

"We're both seeking the truth."

"For different reasons."

"The end result is the same. Oh, and by the way, I may have another victim coming forward."

"Related to Professor Matthews?"

"A former graduate student. Similar story. Said he made unwanted advances, but she felt compelled to sleep with him or suffer repercussions. She needed his recommendation, and she feared he'd withhold it if she didn't comply."

"What's her name?"

"Information is a two-way street, Deputy."

I gave her a look.

"Besides, until she agrees to go public, I'm sworn to secrecy."

"See, we both have vows to keep."

She smirked. "I'll keep you posted, and I know you'll do the same."

She spun around, twirling her wavy blond hair. The smell of her fruity shampoo wafted past my nostrils, briefly obscuring the acrid stench of the smoldering vehicle. I watched her hips sway as she moved back to the crew and plotted their next shot.

We wrapped up at the scene, headed back to the station to fill out reports, then called it a night. My clothes and hair were saturated with the stench of smoke from the blaze. JD dropped me off at the marina, and I hustled down the dock to the *Avventura*. Buddy greeted me eagerly with his slobbering tongue and wagging tail. I took him out for a walk, then I hopped in the shower, letting the sooty grime swirl down the drain.

Isabella called as I was settling in for the evening. "I've got something. It's not much, but it's a start. I checked all the traffic through the cell tower closest to the explosion. A text message was sent from a burner phone to another burner at the time of detonation. That was the triggering event."

"Where did the text originate from?"

"From the GPS data, it looks like that text was sent from a vehicle not even 100 yards behind."

"Ian was following Langston and Dayna," I said.

"Looks that way."

"I'll see if I can find any cameras that may have captured him on the road."

"Have your people subpoena records from the cell provider. They should comply."

"I will. Thanks for the info."

"I'm starting to feel like I work for you instead of the other way around."

I chuckled. "Just one old friend helping another."

"I'll remember that next time I need something."

The next morning, I had Denise go about acquiring the data through legitimate means.

"I'm on it," she said. "Daniels got an arrest warrant for Archer and Cole based on CJ's statement. You want to pick them up now or build the case a little more?"

"It's kinda flimsy at this point, but let's bring them in and see what we can get out of them. Have Erickson, Faulkner, Mendoza, and Robinson meet us at Sandpiper Point in an hour."

"You got it."

I ended the call, ate breakfast, then got in touch with JD. He came over, and we donned our tactical gear, then headed to the marina. From what I could tell, Archer and Cole were full-time live-in bodyguards on Simon Brennan's yacht.

We met up with the other deputies in the parking lot, then made our way down the dock to *Mr. Sparkles*. With our weapons drawn, we rushed across the passerelle and stormed the superyacht.

"Coconut County!" I shouted. "We have a warrant!"

46

The aft deck and salon were empty. I advanced down the starboard side deck with JD. Erickson and Faulkner took the port side, while Mendoza and Robinson remained aft.

The barrel of my pistol led the way as I crept forward down the long passage. The morning sun glimmered the water, and waves lapped against the hull. I climbed the steps to the foredeck, where Simon Brennan sat at a table. It looked like we had interrupted a late breakfast. His two goons were close by.

"Coconut County!" I shouted. "We have a warrant for the arrest of Archer and Cole Lynch."

Simon's face crinkled. "This is preposterous. What have they done?"

"Breaking and entering. We have an eyewitness who saw both Archer and Cole in Fawn DiCarlo's apartment the night of her disappearance and again yesterday."

The two thugs exchanged a concerned glance.

"Put your hands behind your head, and don't make any sudden moves."

Simon nodded to his thugs, and they reluctantly complied. "Are you arresting me as well?"

"Not yet," I said.

Faulkner slapped the cuffs around Archer's wrists and latched them behind his back.

JD advanced to Cole and secured him while I kept my weapon at the ready.

"You have the right to remain silent," JD began.

"Don't say a word," Simon instructed them. "I'll have you out as soon as possible." His annoyed eyes burned into me. "You're making a terrible mistake. Who is this eyewitness?"

I said nothing.

Faulkner and Erickson dragged Archer down the starboard passage, while JD grabbed Cole by his massive bicep and pulled him aft the way we came.

"Care to tell me why your thugs were in Fawn DiCarlo's apartment?" I asked.

"I honestly can't say."

"They were looking for something."

"What my employees do on their personal time is their business. You can't possibly expect me to keep tabs on them 24/7."

"You don't find it the least bit odd that a woman whose services you utilized on a regular basis has gone missing and is likely dead, and your security staff is rummaging through her belongings?"

"I have no comment on the matter, Deputy."

"I know, I know, you're not going to say anything without an attorney."

He stared at me for a moment. "Now that you've executed your warrant, you can remove yourself from my property."

"You want to know what I think?"

"Not particularly."

"I think Fawn DiCarlo stole from you. I think you got mad about it and had her killed."

He chuckled. "You have an active imagination, Deputy. I'll give you that."

"I've got a warrant to search the boat for the key to Fawn DiCarlo's apartment. You don't mind if I look around?"

His face tightened. He minded quite a bit.

I turned the superyacht upside down with Mendoza and Robinson. We had a narrow scope of what we were looking for. I was hoping we'd turn up other contraband in the process, but there was nothing incriminating aboard.

The goons had been stuffed into the back of patrol cars, taken to the station, processed, printed, and put into separate interrogation rooms.

JD and I left the marina and headed to the station. We filled out the requisite paperwork, and by that time, Archer and Cole had been simmering for a while.

Their belongings had been confiscated during processing. I looked over the items and discovered Fawn's apartment key on Archer's keyring. I recognized the distinct style right away. It matched the key I had gotten from the property manager.

I removed the key from Archer's keyring, moseyed down the hall, and pushed into interrogation room #1. JD and I took a seat across the table from Archer. I slapped the key down in front of him.

He glared at us with his cold, narrow eyes, unflinching. Archer wasn't the kind of guy to get frazzled by the situation. He was cool under pressure.

"What were you looking for in Fawn's apartment, besides the kilo of cocaine that she stole from Simon?"

He said nothing.

"Where'd you get the key?" I asked, tapping it.

His brown eyes just stared back at me.

"I think you guys abducted her in the parking lot, ransacked her place, then brought her back to your boss. I mean, a kilo of coke isn't chump change. What's the street value of that now? $35-40K?"

"Depends on the quality," JD said.

"Seems like your boss is dealing in more than just diamonds," I said.

Archer was good at keeping his mouth shut.

"This isn't looking good for you guys. It's only a matter of time before we connect all the dots. You, your brother, and Simon are all going down for kidnapping and murder."

That still didn't seem to faze him.

"Who's tougher?" I asked.

His brow knitted with confusion.

"You, or Cole? Who's tougher? I don't mean physically either. I'm talking about real toughness. Mental toughness."

Archer didn't say anything, but he didn't have to. I could see the answer in his eyes. He knew it, and I knew it.

"You're older. You're the tough one, aren't you? Your baby brother is a little bigger. He's spent more time in the gym. But you're the one who's unbreakable. He's going to sing first. He's gonna cut a deal to save his skin. Hey, I know, blood is thick, but when you're looking at a life sentence..." I shook my head. "I've seen siblings sell each other out on plenty of occasions."

Archer remained stoic, but my words were beginning to creep around in his brain. "You don't know what you're talking about."

At least I got him to say something.

47

Cole put on the tough guy act, too. We took a seat across from him in interrogation room #2, and I tried to see if I could find the cracks in his armor. "You know, I was wrong about you guys."

Cole's brow knitted with curiosity.

We had left him sitting in the room by himself for another hour or so after we interviewed Archer. I wanted to get his mind racing. The longer we kept him waiting, the more he wondered what was going on.

"I figured Archer for the tough one." I let that sit there for a minute.

Cole's eyes flicked between the two of us.

"I'm just gonna put it to you straight. Right now, you're not only looking at breaking and entering. You're looking at kidnapping and murder."

Cole's face tightened. "That's bullshit."

I rolled my eyes. "Save it. Archer already confirmed what we suspected," I lied. "You abducted Fawn in the parking lot. You searched her apartment and recovered some of Simon's property, but not all. You took her back to Simon, and, well, we both know the rest."

The slightest trace of panic filled his eyes. His left eye twitched slightly.

"So, here's the thing. I don't really care about you and Archer. I want Simon. Just confirm what your brother already told us, and that will help us build our case. I'm sure the prosecutor will work out a deal for a very minimal sentence."

His jaw flexed, and his eyes continued to shift between the two of us.

"Is Simon really paying you enough? You're looking at a life-time behind bars. All for what?"

He was silent. A thin mist formed on his brow. I was right. He was the weaker one mentally.

"Do yourself a favor. My offer isn't going to stay on the table forever."

His head dropped, and he stared at the table for a moment. I thought he was getting close to the breaking point, but he looked up at me and summoned his inner strength. "You two can go fuck yourselves."

I lifted an amused brow, then nodded slowly. "Okay. If that's the way you want to play it," I said in an ominous tone. I glanced at JD, then we both pushed away from the table. As I walked toward the exit, I called back over my shoulder, "Enjoy life in prison."

"I'll be out in the morning," he said with confidence.

I knocked on the door, and a guard buzzed us out. We stepped into the hallway.

Jack shook his head. "I thought he was going to spill there for a second."

"You win some. You lose some."

They would be kept in separate cells overnight. They'd be arraigned in the morning. I was sure Simon would post bail.

Paris called. "Hadley Hutton."

"Who's that?"

"The girl I talked to you about. She's coming down to the studio to do an on-camera interview. She said I can release her name to the authorities. She's the one who claims she was coerced into sexual activity with Professor Matthews."

"How did you convince her to go public?"

"You know how persuasive I can be. And I always get what I want."

I couldn't argue with that.

"When did this happen?"

"Last year."

"This is great, but you know there's nothing there. He's going to say it was consensual."

"He's a tenured professor at an acclaimed university in a position of authority over his student. You may not be able to make a case with this one, but I guarantee you, it's going to ruffle feathers. Where there's smoke, there's fire. I have a feeling the floodgates are about to open."

"We'll take a statement from her."

"I'll see you soon."

I ended the call and caught JD up to speed. We headed to the TV studio and found Paris with her crew setting up on the soundstage.

Hadley Hutton was a cute blonde in her late 20s with straight hair, a petite frame, and pretty features. She didn't wear much makeup. She didn't need it. The makeup artist powdered her before she went on camera just to keep the shine down from the heavy lights. She recounted the incident on camera just as Paris had described. It was tearful, just like Mia's story.

Afterward, Hadley came down to the station and made a sworn affidavit.

The interview ran that evening. We happened to catch it on the flatscreen behind the bar at *Diver Down*. Paris came across as compassionate and concerned. She was evolving as a reporter.

We chowed down on seafood enchiladas with rice and beans, washing it down with beer.

Juliana Morgan called me after the segment ended. Before she could say a word, I said, "Still think your colleague is innocent?"

"She's a disgruntled former student who didn't get the grades or the recommendation that she wanted."

"Have you talked with Evan about it?"

"He told me he had a brief encounter with her."

"So he admits to having sex with her?"

"Consensual sex," Juliana said.

"Does he tell you about all his conquests?"

"He only mentioned it at the time because she became disgruntled with her grade, and she felt he should have done more for her."

"He exploited his position," I said.

"That's not how Matthews described it. He said she pursued him and was very aggressive."

"He violated school policy."

"There was no policy against dating students at the time."

"Except for positions of authority," I said.

She sighed. "He used poor judgment. He wouldn't be the first man to do something stupid when there was a lack of blood flow to the brain." She paused. "I think this is a case of an ambitious girl who attempted to use her sexuality to advance her academics and her future career opportunities."

"I still think he's the Coed Killer."

She scoffed. "I believe you're a good cop, Deputy Wild. But you're wrong on this one."

"Time will tell," I said.

"Tell her to meet us at Gingerbread's for a game of pool," JD said.

I looked at him like he was crazy. "I don't think they'll let us back in that place."

"Nonsense." He snatched the phone from my hand. "I really think this is a discussion we should have in person. We're on our way to Gingerbread's. You and Cat should join us. And you can make a case for your friend's innocence."

"I heard you boys really tore up the place," Juliana said.

"Circumstances beyond our control," JD replied.

"I have papers to grade. Lessons to plan."

"All work and no play makes Juliana a dull girl."

"Sorry. Some other time."

"Don't you want to make a case for Professor Matthews?"

"Nothing I say is going to change your mind."

"You give up too easily."

"And perhaps you're too persistent."

"I don't blame you for being scared."

She scoffed. "Scared of what?"

"Having your worldview challenged. And losing at pool."

Juliana laughed. "Ha! No way you could beat me."

"Put your money where your mouth is."

"Like I said, Deputy. Maybe some other time."

"Well, if you decide you've got what it takes, you know where we'll be."

"Good night, Deputy," she said before ending the call.

JD handed the phone back to me. With a confident smile, he said, "She's on the hook."

I gave him a skeptical glance and slipped the phone back into my pocket. "$100 says she doesn't show."

"I'll take that bet," he said, extending his hand.

48

H ayden teased us as we entered the bar. "Look out. Here comes trouble."

I raised my hands innocently as we sauntered to the bar.

"What will it be, gentlemen?"

"Two whiskeys, please," JD said.

Hayden grabbed two glasses, filled them full of amber liquid, and slid them across the counter.

"If you guys come here more often, you might have to enroll in classes," Hayden said.

"I think JD would like to sign up for a certain occult studies class."

"You know, that's a good idea. She could teach me a thing or two."

"Professor Morgan? Students tend not to skip her class," Hayden said. "She can be quite captivating."

"Indeed," JD said. He took a sip of his whiskey. He looked at me and said, "What do you say we get to that tiebreaker. $200, winner takes all?"

"I'll take your money if you're ready to lose."

We took our drinks, shuffled to the back of the bar, and searched for decent cue sticks. There weren't many options left. We were using the only two good ones the other night, and the only ones we hadn't broken were either warped or had bad tips. I chose one and rolled it on the felt to test it out. It didn't really roll. It just kind of flopped over once.

I dropped quarters in the slot, and the balls rolled free.

We lagged for break. I tapped the cue ball, and it rolled from the top tail to the far rail, bounced back, and came within an inch of the near bumper.

Jack's lag fell a little short.

"Make it a tight rack," I said as he pulled the balls from below the table.

I lined up my shot and popped the cue ball, sending it screeching across the felt. It smacked into the one and broke up the balls nicely. They scattered across the table. A solid dropped into the corner pocket and a stripe into the side.

I grinned, and JD frowned at me.

I walked around the table, surveying the layout, then chose to go with solids. I proceeded to knock them down one by one, running the table until I was lining up a shot on the eight-ball.

Jack pouted in the corner, sipping his whiskey.

The eight-ball was against the side bumper, not far from the side pocket. The cue ball was across the table near the opposite bumper. I lined up the shot, drew the stick back, and tapped the cue ball. It rolled across the felt, clacked against the eight, banking the little black ball on target. It launched from the rail and dropped into the opposite side pocket with the sweet sound of money.

JD's face tensed, and he grumbled, "Lucky bastard."

I grinned. "Luck's got nothing to do with it."

The wheels turned behind his eyes, and it wasn't long before he blurted, "One more. Double or nothing."

"If you've got money to burn," I said with a taunting grin.

One game turned into two.

Then three.

Soon, Jack was down $1,600 and ready to roll it all once again.

"At this point, I gotta stop you before you get hurt," I said.

"The only person who's gonna get hurt is you when I find my mojo."

"Better keep looking."

JD scowled at me, headed to the bar, got change, and returned with two more beverages. He dropped quarters into the slot, racked the balls, and I broke with $3,200 on the line.

Nothing fell.

He took a turn, dropped a couple solids, then it went back to me. I dropped two stripes. We exchanged a few more turns, and before long, I was lining up the eight-ball. It was a pretty straightforward shot. The eight-ball was halfway between the side and corner, not far from the rail. I'd made this shot a million times before. It was in my sweet spot. It was comfortable. I could do it in my sleep.

"Corner pocket," I said, calling the shot.

"You sure about that?"

"Positive."

He stood distractingly near the pocket and fiddle-farted around.

I put my left hand on the felt and lined up the shot. I held my breath and drew the cue stick back.

Jack had more money than sense. He'd invested well, and the stuff was like paper to him. Still, I couldn't take $3,200 off my best friend. But I had to make it look good. I struck the cue, and it rolled across the dirty, stained felt. It cut the eight-ball and sent it screaming toward the corner. It hit the inside lip of the pocket and rattled between the edge of the bumpers before rolling out.

JD hooted and clutched at his throat, coughing, "Choke. Choke!"

"Yeah, yeah, don't get too cocky."

He strutted around the table with renewed vigor. "Let me show you how it's done."

He lined up his shot and proceeded to run the table. Ball after ball fell into the pocket with an inevitable clunk. Soon, he was lining up the eight-ball. "Corner pocket," he called.

It was a simple shot. The ball was against the rail, inches from the pocket. The cue-ball was midway down the table. Only a moron could miss this shot. All he had to do was just tap it in.

49

Jack struck the ball with authority.

He cut the eight-ball. It rolled along the rail and dropped in the corner pocket as planned. But the cue-ball bounced off the bumper, then the side bumper, rolled across the felt, and dropped into the far corner pocket.

Whoops!

JD grumbled a few obscenities, and his face reddened. He looked like he was about to break his cue stick in half.

I shrugged innocently. "You had your shot, kid. And now you owe me $3200, plus another $100 on top of that 'cause Juliana didn't show."

He scowled at me. "The night is still young."

It wasn't young.

We played a few more rounds for lower stakes, and I let JD win some of his money back. We tabbed out around midnight, paid for the damages from our previous brawl, and strolled to the Porsche. It was parked around the corner. We hopped in and cruised back to the marina at *Diver Down*. JD dropped me off at the dock, and I told him I'd catch up with him in the morning.

"You got lucky," he said.

"And you didn't." I grinned and hopped out. "I'll expect payment in full shortly."

"I'm good for it."

The engine rumbled as he pulled away and howled as he disappeared into the night.

I took Buddy out for a walk before settling in. In a rare display of affection, Fluffy decided to curl herself up beside me in my bunk. The aloof white cat relinquished her Ice Queen crown from time to time. I was sure she'd go back to ignoring me soon.

The next morning, I got a call from Juliana Morgan just after breakfast. "You got what you wanted. Evan Matthews has been suspended pending the outcome of an investigation."

"What I want is the guy behind bars."

"Regardless of whether he's guilty or not?"

"He's not who you think he is," I said.

"And I'll say the same thing to you. Have a nice day, Deputy," she said in an annoyed tone before ending the call.

JD swung by the marina not long after and picked me up. With a frown, he handed me a fat wad of crisp hundred-dollar bills.

I gloated over my winnings.

"Don't spend it all 'cause I *will* win that back from you."

"Dream on, Scratch," I teased.

He scowled at me.

We headed across the island to rattle Ian Goddard's cage. We didn't have anything solid yet, but I wanted to let him know we'd be breathing down his neck.

His truck was parked in front of his house. We banged on the door, but he didn't answer. The light of the video door-bell activated. I knew he was watching us. I smiled and waved into the lens. "Good morning! Just wanted to let you know we're analyzing the pipe bomb fragments, and we will trace it back to you." I cupped my hand to my ear. "Do you hear that? That's the sound of inevitability."

There was no reply.

I smiled and waved at the camera. "Have a nice day."

We strolled the walkway, pushed through the gate, and climbed into the Porsche.

My phone buzzed with a call from Paris Delaney as Jack pulled away from the curb. "Floodgates officially opened," she said, her voice full of glee. "I got three phone calls from girls with the same story."

"Anything actionable?"

"They all said they felt pressured into having sex with

Matthews. All students at the time or former students who needed his recommendation."

"Send them down to the station to make reports."

"I will. But this is the tip of the iceberg."

"Keep me posted."

"Quid pro quo, Deputy. Quid pro quo."

50

Daniels called in the late afternoon to say that Archer and Cole made bail. "Right now, they're charged with breaking and entering. DA declined to pursue kidnapping charges at this time."

"They had Fawn's apartment key," I said.

"Which they could have found in the lot or somewhere else. Get something more substantial."

"We're on it."

"Simon Brennan is obviously importing something besides diamonds. If we can't get him and his thugs on the kidnapping and murder, maybe we can get them on drug charges. I don't care how we get them off the streets as long as we do. How reliable is that eyewitness of yours?"

"CJ? Hard to say. Enough to get them concerned."

"Stay on top of them. Any idea what else Fawn DiCarlo stole from Simon besides the drugs?"

"I have a few ideas. It's all speculation at this point. And we don't know what was really in that brick. Cocaine, heroin, sugar. We're relying on CJ's testimony."

Daniels sighed. "You've got other resources. Use them."

"Trust me. I am."

I ended the call and dialed Isabella. "I need you to dig into Simon Brennan. I know he's dirty."

"I've checked. Whatever he's doing, he's been smart about it because he's not leaving a paper trail." She paused. "His phone calls are all business, and he's probably using a burner with encrypted messaging for everything else. I've tried to send him spyware, but he's not dumb enough to click on a link in random text messages. I'll keep digging."

We headed to the station, swapped the Porsche for the surveillance van, then drove to *Sandpiper Point*. We found a spot where we could get a good visual on *Mr. Sparkles*. By this time, Archer and Cole were back aboard. They conversed with Simon on the sky-deck.

The late afternoon sun dipped toward the horizon, the day quickly evaporating.

The boss didn't look pleased, gesturing wildly.

We aimed the long-range microphone at the trio and watched the ultra-high-def camera feed. There was a lot of wind noise and interference. But we were able to get faint audio. Their thin, metallic voices filtered through the speaker in the van.

"I told you," Simon growled.

"I know," Archer said, cutting him off. "We tried. He got away. They've obviously got the peeping tom stashed somewhere."

"Where?" Simon asked.

Archer shrugged. "Safe house. Hotel. We'll take care of it."

"No, you won't. You won't do anything. They're gonna be all over you. I need you two to lay low." Simon took a deep breath and tried to calm himself. "I'll take—"

The wind gusted, and the speaker crackled. I couldn't make out what he said.

"—But I need to know one thing," Simon continued. "And I need you both to be perfectly honest with me. Have either of you said anything?"

"No," Archer said. "I'm not stupid."

Simon's eyes flicked to Cole.

"Not a word, other than to tell them to go fuck themselves. They tried to play mind games. They said Archer spilled, but I knew better."

Simon surveyed the two of them carefully. "And the Blue Rain?"

"It's not in the apartment," Archer said. "Maybe the dumb bitch pawned it. Probably didn't know what she had."

Simon's face tightened. "No. If that was out there, floating around, word would be on the street by now."

Simon thought for a moment.

I gave a curious look to JD as we watched the figures on the monitor.

"We can go back to the apartment and look one more time," Archer said.

"Not you two. You two are done. I need you to stay off the radar. I will bring on additional personnel. And I know a specialist who—"

The audio crackled again, and I missed the end of Simon's sentence.

"A contractor? Who?" Archer asked.

"At this point, the less I say, the better." Simon paused. "You keep your mouth shut, you do what I tell you, and you're not going to do any time. If you do, it'll be short, and you'll be handsomely rewarded on the other side." He paused, and the muscles in his jaw flexed. "But if you turn on me, I don't need to tell you what happens."

Simon stormed off the sky-deck.

JD's face crinkled. "What's he talking about, the *Blue Rain*?"

I shrugged and searched the Internet. It was such a generic term that the results were all over the map. I found a movie with the same name, a line of women's clothing, an art gallery, a carwash, a roofing company, and a dozen other possible references.

Then I added another term to my search, and it all became clear. I flipped the phone around and showed JD the results. His eyes widened as he gazed at the screen. "Well, I'll be damned."

"We need to go back to that apartment before the landlord empties it out," I said.

I hopped behind the wheel of the surveillance van and cranked up the engine. We pulled out of the parking lot and headed back to the station.

Along the way, I called CJ at the hotel to check on him. The room phone rang and rang and rang, but he never picked up.

Maybe he was in the shower or using the restroom.

I hung up and called back again a few minutes later as we pulled into the parking lot of the Sheriff's Office.

Again, the phone just rang and rang and rang.

51

I exhaled an irritated breath and dialed CJ's cell phone. He picked up after a few rings. I heard splashing and sloshing in the background and the noises of children playing in the pool.

"What are you doing?"

"Nothing," he said sheepishly.

"What did I tell you? And why is your phone on?"

"I'm just hanging out by the pool drinking a piña colada. What am I supposed to do? Sit in that hotel room all day and all night? I'm about to go bat-shit crazy."

"You realize that Archer and Cole have made bail. They're out on the streets. And Simon is looking to hire someone to kill you."

He was silent for a moment.

"This is serious stuff, CJ. Take the piña colada back to the room and shut your phone off. Stay there and don't leave."

"How are they going to find me here?"

"They could track your phone. Somebody could see you. There are a million ways to find somebody if you look."

"I'm bored out of my mind. You don't understand. There are some hot bitches by the pool here."

"Go back to the room, order room service, watch pay-per-view, watch a porno—I don't care."

"Okay, okay," he whined. "I'm going."

"Now! Do you want to live or die?"

"I want to live. No doubt about it."

"I'm going to have my people track your phone. If it's still on the grid, I'll take care of you myself."

"I'm hanging up now."

I ended the call and dialed Isabella and asked her to make sure that CJ's phone stayed off the grid and to call me if it popped back up.

Jack looked at his watch. "Can you handle the apartment search on your own? I gotta get to band practice."

"Not a problem."

"We'll catch up afterward. I think we should check out Hooch Hut tonight for a change of pace."

"Sounds good to me."

We hopped into the Porsche, and he drove me back to the marina and dropped me off. I hustled down the dock to the *Avventura*, grabbed my helmet and gloves, and ran back to the parking lot. I hopped on my sportbike, pulled on my helmet, and cranked up the engine. I twisted the throttle, and the exhaust rattled an aggressive note that echoed across the lot. I eased out the clutch, rolled out of the parking lot, and turned onto the highway. I twisted the throttle and hugged the tank. The wind whistled around, and I hung on for dear life as I went from zero to the speed of light in a matter of seconds. Riding the crotch rocket was like a cardio routine of its own. It got your heart pumping and high-octane adrenaline flowing.

I zipped over to the *Aegaeon* apartments and parked in the visitor lot. I pulled off my helmet, tossed my gloves inside, and attached it to the bike.

The sun had vanished beyond the horizon, and the grayish-purple sky was quickly fading to black.

The property manager was gone, but I had Fawn's apartment key and key-fob, which granted me access to the lobby. I strolled inside, pressed the call button, and took the elevator. Once inside the apartment, I started combing through the unit inch by inch once again—the drawers, the cabinets, inside the microwave. I checked inside the cups and the bowls in the cupboard. I sifted through the contents of cereal boxes, raisins, nuts, bags of sugar and flour, emptying them out, searching for the Blue Rain. Something no bigger than a quarter but more valuable than almost anything else of its kind.

I worked my way through the kitchen, then the living room, rechecking all of the cushions, checking behind picture frames, and checking the soil of the potted plants.

I pushed into the bedroom and began my search again. I searched the pillows, the nightstand drawers, underneath the mattress again, and the dresser drawers. I sifted through her unmentionables, then moved into the bathroom and checked the medicine cabinet and all of her beauty creams and lotions. I poured all of them out, making a mess, looking for the priceless gem. A rare 61-carat blue diamond that had recently sold at auction to a private collector for $85 million.

A month later, the gem was stolen. It was my guess that the thieves were using Simon to fence the stolen merchandise. A rock like that would be nearly impossible to move on the open market. It would have to be a discrete buyer with plenty of disposable income willing to horde the gem away.

It didn't make any sense to me. You can't tell anybody about it. You can't brag about your acquisition to your friends. It has to stay in a vault where you can admire it, but that's it. If it gets lost or stolen, you can't make an insurance claim. The only person that knows you have it is the person who sold it to you. And odds are, they're coming to steal it again.

Simon Brennan was in the diamond *moving* business. He didn't strike me as a gem thief. Maybe he had bought it outright and was moving it, or maybe he was selling it on consignment. If so, I imagined there was an owner out there that was pretty pissed off about now.

With a gem that valuable, Simon would do anything to get it back. He abducted Fawn, and he probably tortured her in an attempt to extract the location, carving her up with a Sawzall one appendage at a time before tossing her overboard.

It was probably just random chance the shark had nibbled on her leg, then wound up in a fisherman's net. Life is full of strange coincidences. But then again, maybe there is no such thing as coincidence. Maybe everything happens the way it's supposed to.

I had the water running in the sink after I had emptied all the shampoos and creams, washing the residue down the drain. I didn't hear someone enter the apartment. I didn't hear them creep through the living room and into the bedroom. Suddenly, they were in the doorway of the bathroom with a black 9mm in my face—a suppressor attached to the threaded barrel.

52

I recognized the man's cold eyes behind the black ski mask. I looked at him. He looked at me.

I didn't have a lot of time to contemplate the situation. All of this transpired in a microsecond. A blink of an eye.

I don't know if he followed me here with the intention of getting rid of a thorn in his side or if he was the fixer that Simon had hired to clean up Archer's and Cole's mess. It didn't matter because either way, the intention in the man's eyes was clear.

He intended to kill me, right then and there.

His finger squeezed the trigger as I lunged for the weapon, pushing it up and away as it went off. The bullet snapped from the barrel, drilled through the shower curtain, and hit the porcelain tile in the shower stall, exploding bits of debris into the tub.

In the same motion, I drew my pistol from my waistband, but he grabbed my hand and shoved it away before I could aim the pistol at his midsection. I tried to strip his weapon from his hand as he tried to strip my weapon from my hand.

There was no room to maneuver in the tiny space. We struggled between the sink, the bathtub, and the toilet behind me.

I kicked him in the balls. He doubled over, and I finished with a knee to his face, shattering his nose.

He tumbled back, and I stripped both weapons free.

He went for a backup in his waistband. That's when I put two shots into his chest.

Blood erupted from the tunnels of flesh, speckling the floor. He fell back against the tile, his eyes wide. He managed to squeeze off one more shot before life escaped from him. The bullet rocketed toward me and passed between my hip and forearm, smacking the back of the toilet shattering the tank. It cracked into several shards, and the waterfall doused the floor, mixing with his blood.

My heart thudded, and my ears rang from the deafening bangs in the tiny space.

I holstered my weapon, set his firearm on the counter, then stepped over the body and knelt beside him. I felt for a pulse in his neck, but he was long gone. I pulled back the ski mask to reveal what I already knew—Ian Goddard had taken his last assignment.

I called Sheriff Daniels, and before long, the apartment swarmed with forensic investigators, deputies, and the medical examiner.

I caught Daniels up to speed when he arrived. He shook his head when he looked at the mess.

"Did you find what you were looking for?"

I shook my head.

"And you think Simon hired him?"

I nodded.

He sighed. "You know the drill. Surrender your duty weapon. You're on administrative leave, pending investigation."

It was standard operating procedure. Usually, we got the day off, had a chat with the head shrinker, then were reinstated.

Brenda examined the remains. The investigators documented the scene, chronicled the bullet hits, and retrieved slugs, calculating the angles. Everything would be used to corroborate my statement.

We continued searching for the Blue Rain, but it wasn't in the apartment. Fawn could have put it into a safety deposit box or hidden it in a storage unit. There was no telling where the precious gem could be.

We wrapped up at the scene, and I headed to the station, filled out an after-action report, made an official statement, and Daniels asked me more questions. It was about that time when I got a call from JD. "Where the hell are you? We're at the Hooch Hut. Get your ass over here."

"You missed all the fun," I said.

I filled him in on the situation.

"You okay?"

"Yeah, I'm good."

"I can't let you do anything by yourself, can I?" JD teased.

"I'm going to call and check on CJ, then I'll meet you at the bar."

"There are plenty of hotties in this place, let me tell you."

I chuckled. "I'll see you in a bit."

I ended the call and dialed the *Seven Seas* again. The receptionist put me through to CJ's room. We booked him in under a false name. It rang and rang and rang.

I grew both concerned and irritated.

I dialed his cell phone, and it went to voicemail after three rings. I figured he probably wouldn't take a call from me, even if the phone was turned on and within arm's reach.

I dialed the hotel again and asked the desk to connect me with CJ's room again.

Still no answer.

Now I was growing concerned.

I found Daniels amid the bustling chaos of the office. "I can't get in touch with CJ."

He shrugged.

"In light of recent events, I'm going to do a welfare check. Simon could have hired Ian Goddard to pay him a visit before he crossed paths with me."

"You're on leave," Daniels said. "I'll send Erickson and Faulkner. I don't need you involved in any more incidents tonight."

"You know you're gonna reinstate me in the morning. Might as well do it now."

"Yes, but it looks bad when you kill more than one person in a day."

"I'm not gonna kill anybody for the rest of the day. I promise. Send Erickson and Faulkner with me, if you want. You know I'm just gonna stop by on my own, anyway."

A resigned sigh escaped his stern lips. "Why do I put up with you two?"

I shrugged.

He stared at me a long moment, then relented. "Go!"

53

I hopped on the bike and cruised to the *Seven Seas*. I met Erickson and Faulkner in the parking lot. I had a spare key to the room, so we headed straight to the second floor and found room #210.

The sounds coming from the hotel room told me that CJ wasn't in any trouble, and I understood exactly why he had been ignoring the phone calls.

Moans of ecstasy seeped out of the room, and a mattress squeaked.

Erickson and Faulkner laughed, then turned around and left, their services no longer needed.

"Call us when you've got a real crime, Wild," Erickson muttered as he strolled back down the hallway to the elevators.

I banged on the door. "Open up, CJ."

The grunting and groaning continued.

"Finish it up!" I shouted after banging again.

The activity crescendoed, then the room went silent. Commotion inside filtered through the door, and a moment later, CJ opened the door wearing a bathrobe.

I stood there, arms folded, giving him a stern gaze. "What did I say about visitors?"

"I don't have any visitors," he stammered.

My eyes narrowed at him.

"I was watching a movie," he said innocently.

I pushed open the door the rest of the way and stepped down the foyer into the room.

I recognized the girl in his bed, covering herself with the sheets—the blonde we had met in the bar, Ashley. She cringed when she saw me. "Am I in trouble?"

A frustrated breath escaped my lips, and I glared at CJ.

He smiled and shrugged innocently. "I just went to the bar for one drink. It was love at first sight." His eyes flicked adoringly to Ashley.

"Love at first sight, huh?"

"I mean, you're not going to deny a man a chance at true happiness, are you?"

"She's a working girl, CJ."

He acted innocent. "You mean, I've got to pay?"

"Goddamn right you do," Ashley said. "I better not get stiffed. You think I fuck trolls like you for fun?"

CJ tightened his jaw, and his body stiffened.

Ashley's eyes flicked to me. She cringed again. Realizing she was trying to conduct business in front of a deputy.

"I'm going to step into the hallway for a minute. You two transact whatever you need to transact, and I'm going to pretend I didn't see any of it." I looked at Ashley. "Then you need to get dressed and go." My angry gaze snapped to CJ. "And you need to get in line with the program."

CJ raised his hands in surrender. "I'm with the program."

"Could have fooled me," I said as I brushed past him and stepped outside, allowing the couple some privacy. I waited in the hallway while they collected themselves. Ashley emerged a few minutes later with an irritated look on her face. "We have a problem."

I closed my eyes and clenched my fists, trying not to erupt. "What kind of problem?"

"His credit card got declined."

I looked at her, incredulous. "That's not my problem."

"I've got rent to pay. This is not cool."

"Maybe you should vet your clients more thoroughly before-hand. Take payment upfront."

"I usually do. But people that stay in this hotel typically have good credit. This place ain't cheap."

"What do you want me to do about it?"

"I want you to make him pay," she said.

"I'm not your pimp."

She lifted a brow, then smirked. "You could be."

I growled, about to explode. "I don't have time for this nonsense. Do you want to go to jail?"

"This is theft of service. He stole from me." She smiled at me again and batted her baby blues, her long lashes flicking up and down. "Besides, you don't really want to take me to jail, do you?" Her eyes fluttered again in seductive ways. "I could make it worth your while. We could have fun."

"I'm going to give you five minutes to go back in there to work things out. I don't want to hear any more about it. I'm tempted to take both of you to jail."

She made a pouty face and turned out her bottom lip.

"Go!"

She pushed back into the room.

CJ poked his head out a moment later and flashed a tentative smile. The kind of smile that told me he was about to ask for a favor.

"What is it?" I asked, my patience expired.

"Can I borrow some money?"

My face tensed, and my eyes rounded. I stared at him like he was nuts. "How much?"

"Just $200. The rest will fit on my card."

I scowled at him. "I'm not paying for a hooker. That wasn't part of the arrangement."

"I'll pay you back."

"Come on, help a brother out."

At that point, I was willing to do whatever it took to make the situation go away. I dug into my pocket, pulled out my money clip, and peeled off two crisp hundred-dollar bills.

CJ's eyes rounded at the size of the wad I had in my pocket, fresh with money JD had given me from his loss.

"Shit. I should have asked for more."

54

I rode the bike back to the marina at *Diver Down*, dropped it off, and caught a cab to meet JD and the band at the *Hooch Hut*. I knew better than to have a few whiskeys and get on a motorcycle. That was a recipe for disaster.

The *Hooch Hut* had a bar downstairs with every imaginable brand of spirit. The deck out back had white Adirondack wooden chairs, tables with umbrellas and blue wooden barstools, and reclaimed wood coffee tables—all shrouded by palm trees. Upstairs, you could lounge in comfy couches and chairs.

We hung out on the patio and listened to a guy strum an acoustic guitar. The place had a cool vibe, and there was plenty of eye candy, though nothing like *Tide Pool*.

The rumble of two loud Harleys rattled outside—the exhaust frapping. It shook the entire building and drowned out the singer on the small stage. I didn't think much of it until Red and Jet staggered onto the deck a few minutes later, amber longnecks dangling from their grasp.

I nudged JD and subtly pointed.

The two burly bikers hadn't seen us yet.

"Your friends are here," I said.

JD's face tightened. "You ready for trouble?"

"Always."

It didn't take them long to see us and amble in our direction.

JD and I were on our feet by the time they arrived, ready for a confrontation.

"Easy there, boys," Red said. "We're not looking for trouble."

I regarded him with a healthy dose of skepticism.

"You didn't press charges," Red said. "That was pretty cool."

"We're cool guys when you get to know us," JD said.

"What are you two drinking?"

"Whiskey."

Red flagged down a passing waitress. "Sweetie, could you bring my two friends your best whiskey and put it on my tab."

She smiled. "Certainly."

Red extended his hand as the waitress sauntered away. "Thorsten Jamison," he said. "But my friends call me Thor. You met Billy."

We all shook hands and exchanged pleasantries.

"I hope we didn't hurt you too bad the other day," Thorsten said.

Jack wiggled his jaw. "It's still a little tender. You've got a pretty mean left hook."

Thorsten chuckled. "Shit. We hadn't gotten our asses kicked like that in a long time. I guess it's good for the soul. A little reminder to stay humble." He sipped his beer.

I chuckled. "Maybe, but I try to avoid getting my ass kicked whenever possible."

"Something tells me that doesn't happen too often."

"What brings you to Coconut Key?"

"A little fun in the sun. We thought we'd come down and enjoy all the island has to offer. We visited with the chapter brothers, but we've been on our own mostly."

We had a few drinks with the bruisers. They weren't so bad once you got to know them. The Savage Barbarians were a rough and tumble group, as these guys had proven. But the local chapter took it to another level with drugs, kidnapping, and murder. I wasn't sure what, if any, involvement these two had in the gang's illicit activities. Sometimes, just a few bad apples are involved in nefarious schemes. Other times, the entire club is rotten to the core.

I didn't mention my previous run-ins with the outlaw gang.

We thanked Thorsten and Billy for the drinks and called it an early night. The guys in the band were looking to have an after-party on the boat, but I nixed any talk of that right away. I just wanted to crawl in bed and recharge.

We told the guys we'd catch up with them later, and I left with JD. We walked the sidewalk filled with listing revelers and colorful lights. It wasn't quite closing time just yet, and the strip was still lively. Music from bands spilled into the street, and the smell of food from restaurants and street vendors drifted through the air.

We grabbed pizza by the slice from a corner vendor and filled our bellies.

Fat and happy, we headed down Nighthawk Lane, where Jack had parked the Porsche. We climbed in and headed back toward the marina. We cruised with the top down, the stars flickering above, and '80s classics pumping through the speakers.

JD turned onto Woodstar Street. It was a two-lane road with a double yellow line and occasional shoulder parking. There were residential homes, tall palms, and white fences.

Blinding lights from an SUV behind us flooded the cab and bounced off the rearview mirror, squinting JD's eyes. His face twisted into a scowl. "Go around, jackass!"

We were just cruising along in no particular hurry.

The SUV behind us pulled around, and its V8 rumbled. The black behemoth roared alongside. I figured it was a couple of drunk kids, and I planned to give them an annoyed glare as they passed.

But these weren't kids out having too much fun.

An Uzi emerged from the open passenger window.

My eyes rounded, and my heart leaped into my throat.

Muzzle flash flickered from the barrel, and a stream of molten copper sprayed.

JD and I ducked as bullets peppered the vehicle. Metal popped and pinged. The windshield webbed with cracks as the spray continued.

I drew my pistol and returned fire.

Sheet metal crinkled as the SUV slammed into the driver's side and ran us toward the curb.

There went the new paint job.

We crossed over the white line into the shoulder that was dotted with parked cars. The right side of the Porsche clipped the left rear of a champagne-colored Lexus, triggering both airbags, spinning the Porsche, bringing us to a sudden and uncomfortable adjustment in speed. Glass and plastic shattered, and the hood accordioned. My safety belt cut into my hips and shoulders, and the impact knocked the breath from my lungs. The airbag felt like a punch to the face, and the pop was deafening. Shards of glass scattered about. Tires squealed.

I bounced around between the seat bolsters as the car spun, finally screeching to a stop.

The crash had knocked the sense out of me, and it took a moment to catch my bearings. My heart pounded, and adrenaline flooded my veins.

I didn't think anything was broken, but I'd be sore as hell in the morning.

I glanced at JD. He looked dazed, and his long blond hair was tousled. He looked down at his chest and clutched his rib cage. When he pulled his hand away, it was covered in crimson blood. "I think I got shot."

The SUV was long gone.

The thugs had raced to the next intersection and rounded the corner, disappearing into the night. The assailants wore ski masks, and there were no plates on the vehicle. But I'd wager all the money left in my pocket that Simon Brennan was behind this.

I dialed 911 and requested emergency services as I hopped out of the vehicle and rushed around the other side to attend to JD. I told him to keep pressure on the wound, and he did.

Other cars had stopped, and headlights from both directions illuminated the crumpled Porsche. Smoke from the tires still wafted in the air, drifting through the shafts of light.

JD looked a little pale and woozy, and the color was draining from his face.

"Hang in there, Buddy. You're gonna be okay. Just breathe."

He took a breath and nodded.

"How bad is it?"

"It's not good."

The fact that he was still conscious and had a sense of humor was a good sign. But I'd be lying if I said I wasn't worried.

55

Red and white lights flickered from the ambulance. EMTs and paramedics stabilized Jack, started him on oxygen and an IV drip, and loaded him into the back of the meat wagon.

Red and blues from patrol cars danced. Wreckers hovered nearby, waiting like vultures to claim the wreckage. Shattered glass and plastic sparkled like diamonds on the asphalt. A curious crowd of onlookers gawked.

The rotor blades of Tango One pattered overhead. Its spotlight slashed the night, illuminating the wreckage.

Paris Delaney and her news crew had arrived on the scene, along with several other stations.

We exchanged a glance as I climbed aboard the ambulance with JD.

"You're gonna be okay, Brother," I assured. "You're in good hands."

Jack looked up at me and nodded, his breath fogging the oxygen mask. There was more than a little concern behind those eyes.

"We've got a lot more hell to raise. Don't get any funny ideas about going anywhere."

"I ain't going nowhere," he said with a wince.

When you get wheeled into the ER with a gunshot wound, they take it pretty seriously. They don't make you wait around with all the other sick and suffering. They triage you and take you straight back.

I hovered nearby as the medical team worked frantically to evaluate Jack's condition. A *Focused Assessment with Sonography for Trauma* was done (FAST). A nurse drew blood, and Dr. Parker examined the wound. "I thought I told you last time never to come back again."

"I've been trying to stay away."

"Not very hard, apparently."'

Dr. Parker hunched over JD's bloodied and bruised torso, poking and prodding around the entry wound.

The bullet had pierced the door, drilled through the internals and the interior leather, and smacked into JD's rib cage. It hit one of his ribs and fractured the bone, lodging in one of the intercostal muscles. All things considered, he'd gotten pretty lucky.

Dr. Parker tried to palpate the bullet with his index finger. "There it is. I feel it."

JD winced. Through clenched teeth, he said, "So do I. Can you not do that?"

"Can you stop getting shot?"

Dr. Parker dug around with a pair of forceps. After some doing, he pulled out the bullet and the larger bone fragments.

"Save that for me," Jack said as Parker dropped the mangled slug onto a specimen tray with a clank. "I want to add it to my collection."

"Must be getting pretty large by now," Parker quipped.

"It is."

"You're lucky your intercostal artery wasn't lacerated."

Dr. Parker irrigated the wound and debrided the damaged tissue. They sent JD off for a CT scan after he'd been patched up to make sure there was no internal bleeding and no other bullets and bone fragments anywhere.

A nurse urged me to get evaluated. I looked pretty battered. But I declined.

Jack was admitted to the hospital for observation overnight. A couple of nurses transferred him to the trauma ward, rolling his bed down the antiseptic hallways and up the patient elevator.

We settled into his private room. JD's vital signs beeped on the monitor beside the bed. An IV bag hung from a stand. There was a flatscreen TV on the wall near the ceiling and a chair that folded out into a *sleeper*—and I use the term lightly. The window looked out over the parking lot.

They had JD pretty dosed up on pain meds, so he wasn't feeling much—except when he coughed, or laughed, or tried to move.

I tried to make myself comfortable in the recliner.

"You don't need to stick around," JD said. "There's no point."

"Somebody just tried to kill us. That's twice in one day for me."

"I think it was a subtle hint for us to lay off the investigation," JD said.

"Good thing we don't take subtle hints well."

He grinned. "I'm going to go out on a limb and say that Simon is responsible. Did you get a look at the guys in the vehicle?"

"I was a little distracted by the bullets. They wore ski masks, as I recall. They were big guys. Could have been Archer and Cole. Could have been somebody else. We know Simon is willing to hire outside of his organization to get things done."

"Right now, I'm of the mind we just take care of this our way," JD said.

Our way meant to hell with the rules—just take the bastard out. There was a time in my life where I would have done just that. But I was really trying not to kill people unless it was absolutely necessary. There was certainly an argument to be made that this was necessary.

"We'll get that son-of-a-bitch," I said. "One way or another."

"That's what I like to hear."

"I guess this means we need to cancel the upcoming show."

JD's face crinkled. "Nonsense."

"I don't think you're going to be in any condition to sing."

"I've sung with broken ribs before. There's nothing more rock 'n' roll than getting on stage and singing a few days after you've been shot."

He smiled.

"You want me to call Scarlett?"

JD shook his head. "No sense upsetting her." He paused. "On second thought, maybe she needs to have a little sympathy for her old man. Might make her realize life can change at any minute. Don't take a second for granted."

I pulled out my phone and dialed Scarlett's number.

"Play it up a little," JD whispered.

Scarlett was three hours behind on the West Coast. She answered after a few rings, and I put the call on speaker. "Hey, Tyson. What's up?"

I heard music and commotion in the background. "Where are you at?"

"I'm at a party, but I swear I'm not drinking. Are you checking up on me?"

"No, I've got some news," I said in a somber tone.

"What kind of news?" she asked, her voice cautious.

"Everything's okay. But I just thought you should know, JD's been shot."

"What!?"

"He's okay. He's been treated and admitted to the hospital."

"Is he all right?" she asked, her voice tightening.

"He got lucky. He's a little black and blue. But I think he's gonna live."

"I'm on the next plane out," she said.

"I'm sure he'd love to see you."

"What happened?"

"I'll let him tell you all about it." I handed the phone to Jack.

"Hey, sweetheart," he said, then proceeded to fill her in on all the details.

A replay of Paris's report from the scene played on the flatscreen. The sound was muted, but the pictures said it all.

JD cringed when he saw the images of the Porsche. It looked even worse than I remembered. Something told me there'd be no salvaging it this time.

Juliana Morgan called on the other line while Jack was still talking to Scarlett. "I gotta take this call, but I'll see you soon." He clicked over to Juliana. "Isn't it past your bedtime?"

"JD?"

"In the flesh."

"Why are you answering Tyson's phone? Is he okay?"

"He'll survive. I'm the one you should be worried about."

"They said on the news a deputy was taken to the hospital and is in critical but stable condition," she said, her voice full of worry.

"I got a few more holes in me than I had before, but otherwise, I'm doing okay."

"You got shot!?"

"Hazards of the job."

"And Tyson?"

"Lucky bastard didn't get a scratch."

"I got a few scratches," I said, the bruising from the seat belt starting to settle in.

"But you're both going to be alright?"

"Is that concern I hear?" JD asked.

"Professional concern. Nothing more, I can assure you."

"Well, either way, I appreciate the call."

"Is there anything you need? Anything I can do for you?"

JD's eyes filled with lewd thoughts. "Oh, there are quite a few things I need."

"Medically related," she clarified.

"Not at the moment, but I'll take a rain check."

"Good night, Deputy. Speedy recovery."

He ended the call and was going to hand the phone back to me, but I didn't feel like getting off the recliner at the moment.

Teagan called an instant later to get the scoop and make sure he was okay. They talked for a few minutes, and I told Jack to ask her to take care of Buddy and Fluffy tonight. She had a key to the boat and was always eager to spend time with the fur-balls.

Denise called not long after. Jack put it on speaker, and she informed us, "They found the black SUV a few blocks from the crash site. It had been stolen. The shooters set it on fire. Investigators weren't able to recover any usable evidence."

"Figures."

The forensics guys found a few shell casings in the street. Maybe they'll get lucky and pull a print. They were also able to pull a few slugs from the car. With any luck, ballistics will get a match. Sorry about the Porsche."

"I am too."

A surprising figure appeared at the door to the room. "I hope I'm not disturbing anything."

My face tensed.

56

P aris Delaney's delightful figure was silhouetted in the doorway by the fluorescent lights in the hall. The lighting in JD's room was dim. I looked beyond the gorgeous blonde for her camera crew, but I didn't see them.

"I'm not here in a professional capacity," she said. "I just wanted to make sure you both were okay."

She stepped into the room, and my annoyed expression faded.

She looked at JD and waved while he still talked to Denise. He'd taken the call off speaker and now had the phone to his ear.

"How are you feeling?" she asked me.

"Like I got stepped on by an elephant."

She cringed. "That doesn't sound fun. You guys are lucky to be alive."

I agreed.

"He looks good, all things considered," she said, nodding to Jack.

"He'll probably outlive us all. Charmed life."

"You both seem pretty charmed," she said with a smile. "Are you going to stay here all night with him?"

I nodded.

"You think somebody might make another attempt on your lives?"

"Maybe not tonight, but somebody is figuring out that we're a pain in the ass."

She chuckled. "You know who?"

"This is starting to sound like an interview?"

She huffed, and her eyes narrowed at me. "Personal curiosity. I told you, I'm not working right now." Paris was always working. She reached out and grabbed my hand affectionately. "Whatever you may think about me, I do have a heart, Deputy."

"I appreciate your concern."

We looked into each other's eyes for a long moment. Her concern seemed genuine.

"Well, I really should be going." She paused. "You're not going to sleep in this chair all night, are you?"

"That's the plan."

"What's the old saying... No plan ever survives the battlefield?"

I laughed. "This chair just might win."

"I'm glad you both are okay. Good night, Deputy."

She sauntered to the door, and I watched her silhouette sway. She waved again before disappearing into the hallway. Even the hardened reporter had a soft interior. You just had to peel away a few layers to get to it.

I fought against the chair all night. The nurses came in to do checks at all hours. There was no getting a decent night's sleep in a place like this.

By the morning, I was stiff and sore. I felt it in my neck, my back, my hips, and in muscles I didn't even know I had. There was a purple bruise across my chest in the shape of a seatbelt that was yellow around the edges.

Erickson and Faulkner stopped by to see how Jack was doing. They said they'd stick around a while and keep an eye on things. I didn't think Simon would send his goons to finish the job in broad daylight, but you never know. The best time to attack is when it's least expected.

I used the opportunity to duck out. I wanted to get home, take a shower and eat a real breakfast. I wasn't sure when JD would be getting discharged. They had made some noise like they might let him go in the afternoon, but I couldn't get any straight answers.

I asked JD if he wanted anything before I left. I told him I'd bring back a pair of clothes and a phone charger. He asked me to sneak in a little whiskey, but I had to be the voice of reason.

I called for a rideshare back to *Diver Down*.

On the boat, I got cleaned up and changed, and was about to fix breakfast when Daniels called. "Got a call from a guy who says he witnessed Fawn's abduction in the parking lot. Said he was a little hesitant to come forward at first. Apparently, his business partner's wife was blowing him in the parking lot in his car when the incident took place. He's on his way down to the station now to look at mugshots."

"I'll be right there."

I threw a breakfast burrito in the microwave, chowed it down, grabbed my helmet and gloves, and jogged to the parking lot. I hopped on the bike and zipped down to the station.

Travis Walsh arrived 20 minutes later. He was an average-looking guy in his 30s with a round face and short brown hair. He was a little soft around the midsection. At first glance, he didn't look like the type of guy that was melting panties. But to listen to him talk, he was killing it.

Probably exaggeration.

"I'll stay completely anonymous, right?" Travis asked.

"You may have to testify at some point," Daniels said.

His face tensed with concern. "See, this is why I didn't say anything. Nobody can find out about this."

"These people killed a girl, and they attempted to kill two of my deputies."

"You're doing the right thing," I assured.

His face crinkled with torment. "I mean, this is my best friend's wife. He can't find out."

"Are you sure you understand the definition of *best friend*?" I asked.

He glared at me. "Look, she came on to me. What am I supposed to do?"

"Did she see anything?"

"No. She was a little preoccupied if you know what I mean. She didn't come up for air until after they were gone. I told her about it afterward, but we both decided to keep our mouths shut."

"Why the change of heart?"

He shrugged. "I don't know. I saw the story about the girl and the shark. The report said she was kidnapped from the apartment complex. I knew it had to be the same girl."

We showed him several mugshots of random inmates, including Archer and Cole. He picked Archer out right away. "Yeah, that's him."

"You sure about that?"

"Positive."

He picked out Cole as well.

With Travis's sworn affidavit, we were able to get a warrant.

"These are ruthless individuals," Daniels said to Travis. "You may be in danger if your identity becomes known."

Travis's eyes rounded. "What!? Now you tell me."

"We can offer you protection if necessary."

"Do you think it's necessary?" he asked with concern.

"It's rare that bail would be granted in a kidnapping case," Daniels said. "If it is, it would be high."

"You'll let me know if these guys get sprung, right?"

I nodded.

He thought for a moment. "And nobody's gonna know I said anything unless it goes to trial, right?"

"Theoretically," I said.

"What do you mean, *theoretically*?"

"Shit happens."

"I don't like the sound of that."

"We can put you in a safe location," Daniels said.

"I got a business to run. I can't sit in a safe house. These things can take forever to go to trial." He groaned. "See, this is why I didn't want to get involved." He frowned at us. "I'm going home. If these guys get back out on the street after you pick them up, let me know."

"We'll keep you posted."

Travis marched out of the station, and we headed over to *Sandpiper Point* with Mendoza and Robinson. Erickson and Faulkner met us there, and we all stormed *Mr. Sparkles*.

"Coconut County!" I shouted as we boarded the boat, weapons drawn. "We have a warrant!"

57

The deputies fanned out. I took the starboard side passage to the foredeck while Mendoza and Robinson searched the salon. Daniels followed me. Erickson and Faulkner took the port side.

We converged on Simon, eating breakfast at the settee on the foredeck.

Three new thugs stood at his side. They were even bigger than Archer and Cole. Muscle-heads. Walking tanks. Dudes with square jaws and thick necks that disappeared into giant shoulders. Boulders for biceps. They all wore dark sunglasses, and their bodies tensed as we surrounded them. They were armed with pistols holstered in their waistbands.

They raised their hands in surrender. Deputies storming the boat with weapons drawn made a pretty convincing argument to comply peacefully.

"Deputy Wild, what a pleasant surprise," Simon said with an insincere tone.

"Where are Archer and Cole?"

"In light of recent circumstances, I asked them to tender their resignations. I can't be associated with potential criminals."

I scoffed and nodded to the bodyguards. "New hires?"

"Yes, and so far, they are doing an excellent job."

"So, you have no idea where Archer and Cole may be?"

"I terminated their employment and gave them a generous severance package. I asked them to leave my boat immediately. I'm sorry I can't be of more help."

I wanted to smack the smug grin from his face.

Erickson and Faulkner joined us moments later.

"They're not here," Faulkner said.

"Sorry you wasted your time, Deputies," Simon said. "Good luck in your search."

I glared at him. "Your assassination attempt last night failed. We are both still alive."

"I'm afraid you're confused. I appreciate your commitment to your job. Your fervor to seek justice. But you're on the wrong track. And, if I'm being frank, this is bordering on harassment. I don't know why you're obsessed with me. I'm an honest businessman, just trying to make a living."

I smiled. "No, you're a drug dealer and a fence."

"Those are bold allegations."

"Fawn DiCarlo stole the Blue Rain from you."

That got his attention. He tried to cover, acting ignorant. "I don't understand. The Blue Rain?"

I chuckled. "Please. You're an international diamond dealer, and you're not familiar with the Blue Rain?"

"Ah, yes. Stolen not long ago from a European collector, if I recall correctly. You'd have to be a fool to go anywhere near that diamond. Way too hot."

"Someone with your connections could move it. A private collector somewhere."

Simon smiled. "I'm glad you think so highly of me, Deputy. But none of my clients would touch that stone." He smirked. "You do have quite the imagination, though."

"You can stop with the charade," I said. "I don't know who you were moving the stone for, but I'm guessing you're pretty desperate to get it back. You're gonna have to cough up the stone or $85 million. Otherwise, the owner is going to take it out of your ass. Am I right?"

"No, you are not right. Now, if you'll excuse me, I would like to enjoy my morning in private."

"My friend is in the hospital because of your goons. And I'm not going to stop until you're dead or behind bars."

"Are you threatening me?"

I shook my head calmly. "No. Just telling you like it is."

Simon looked at Daniels. "You really need to reign in your deputy. He's out of line."

"Alright, boys. It's time to roll." Daniels forced a pleasant face. "We apologize for the inconvenience."

We left *Mr. Sparkles* and regrouped on the dock.

Paris Delaney waited with her crew. Someone had tipped her off, and she had planned on capturing the takedown.

Daniels said, "I'll put a BOLO out on those two dirtbags, but something tells me we're not going to find them."

"They were the only ones that could connect Fawn's murder to Simon," I said.

"I think they're shark food," Faulkner quipped.

"I tend to agree with you," Daniels replied. His steely gaze found me. "Hurry up and get something on this guy."

"I'm trying."

We had a vague conversation recorded between Simon, Archer, and Cole on the sky-deck. That was it. It was a conversation we didn't have a warrant to obtain, and the courts would likely rule the goons had a *reasonable expectation of privacy* aboard the boat. The Sheriff's Department had limited authority to check boats for document and safety compliance. Recording warrantless conversations was beyond the scope.

We walked toward the lot, and I stopped to chat with Paris. "Sorry, no show today."

She frowned. "Maybe I can get an interview with Simon."

"Doubtful."

"Even if he tells me to fuck off on camera, it's useable. I just need a clip to go with the story."

We both looked at the superyacht. Simon and his goons stood on the foredeck watching us. I waved and smiled just to annoy him.

"You think he's responsible for Fawn DiCarlo's death?"

"I do."

"And last night's attack?"

"That's a good bet."

I caught her up to speed. She got excited when I mentioned the blue diamond.

"This is getting juicy!"

"Don't get too excited. We've got nothing solid on the guy."

She smirked. "Leave it to me. I'll dig up something."

I chuckled. "I'm sure you will."

I jogged to the lot and caught up with the guys while Paris and her crew hustled toward *Mr. Sparkles* to get a statement.

58

I filled out after-action reports at the station, then went back to *Diver Down*. I took a seat at the bar and tried not to look glum—hard to do when your best friend is in the hospital and the scumbag responsible is sitting pretty.

"How's JD doing?" Teagan asked.

"He's getting along okay. Thanks for taking care of Buddy and Fluffy last night."

She smiled. "Anytime. Can I get you anything?"

"Diet soda."

She grabbed a glass, filled it full of ice, then poured from the fountain. She slid the drink across the counter, and I sipped on it as I contemplated the recent events. I stared at the fish tank, which was now behind the bar, watching the colorful occupants glide about. It was a soothing, relaxing view.

"Corbin got the tank setup. Sorry, I forgot to call you. It looks good, don't you think? Several customers commented on it. Are we going to keep it?"

"Unless I can find a better home for them."

She smiled.

They say a fish tank will lower your blood pressure. I'm not sure about that, but it did seem to have a calming effect.

Then I saw it.

I launched from the barstool and moved around the counter. I crouched down and looked through the glass at the fake coral and the treasure chest full of gems and pearls.

There it was.

The sparkling blue diamond. The 61-carat, flawless *Blue Rain*.

I couldn't believe I never noticed it before. It was right there in plain sight the whole time.

I reached my arm into the tank, and the fish scattered. My fingers grasped the blue diamond, and I pulled it from the treasure chest. Water dripped from my arm onto the floor.

"What is it?" Teagan asked.

I glanced around the bar to see who was watching. Harlan sat at the far end, sipping his beer, staring right at me.

"It's nothing," I said.

"That doesn't look like *nothing*," she said, surveying the sparkling stone.

$85 million in the palm of my hand.

I grabbed a napkin and dried my arm and the stone, then slipped it into my pocket.

"Is that real?" she asked in a hushed tone.

"No," I said.

Her face tensed. "Why are you putting it in your pocket?"

"Because it's too pretty to sit in the bottom of the tank."

She wasn't buying it for a second. "Don't lie to me. You know I can sense these things."

I leaned in and whispered in her ear. Her eyes rounded as I told her the story.

"Holy shit! You mean that's been sitting there the whole time?"

"Maybe you could talk a little louder."

Her teal eyes narrowed at me.

Harlan's curious eyes continued to survey us. "You think I can get another beer if it's not too much trouble?"

"Coming right up," Teagan said.

"Say a word to no one," I muttered to her.

"Better make that two if you want me to keep my mouth shut," Harlan said.

"Give him two on the house."

Teagan popped the top off two long necks and delivered them to the old Marine.

"One at a time, Sugar," Harlan said with a grin.

She took one back and kept it on ice for him.

Teagan made her way back to me and whispered, "What are you going to do with that?"

"Use it as bait."

59

Having an $85 million diamond in your pocket was an unusual sensation. I certainly didn't want to lose it.

It could buy a lot of things. A nice superyacht, dozens of exotic cars, luxurious houses. But we already had a pretty nice superyacht. Then there was the pesky little problem of moving the stone. There were a lot of compelling arguments for keeping it. But none that rivaled seeing Simon Brennan behind bars.

I left *Diver Down* and walked back to the *Avventura*, keeping my hand in my pocket, wrapped around the jewel. I pushed into the salon, pulled out my phone, and dialed Simon. He answered after a few rings. "Simon. Buddy! How are you doing?"

"How much longer is this harassment going to continue?"

"I'm not harassing you. I swear. I just wanted to tell you I've got what you're looking for."

"I'm not looking for anything."

"You sure about that?" I pulled the diamond from my pocket and held it up to a shaft of light that beamed through the windows. I gazed at the gem's hypnotic sparkle. The clarity. The sheer perfection of the stone. "Right now, I am looking at the most luxurious blue diamond that I have ever seen. Granted, I haven't seen a lot of blue diamonds, but this thing is damn nice."

Simon said nothing.

"Want to know where I found it?"

"It's not every day one stumbles across a blue diamond."

"In the fish tank of all places. Can you believe your goons searched Fawn's apartment and didn't bother to look in the fish tank? I mean, I didn't think to look until just now. And it's a good thing I did. It just kind of jumped out at me."

I let that hang there for a moment.

"But hey, since it's not yours, and you didn't lose it, I guess there's no point in my calling. Have a nice day, Simon."

I was about to hang up when the dirtbag said, "You like to play games, don't you?"

"Keeps me entertained."

"Well, I don't think you're going to like this one," he said in an ominous tone before he hung up.

I had no doubt Simon would send his goons after the diamond. It was just a question of when.

I figured they wouldn't attack in broad daylight. They'd wait till the wee hours of the morning, and I'd be ready and waiting.

JD called, and I caught him up to speed. He seemed mildly amused but was more concerned with another matter. "You're not gonna believe this crap. They want to keep me for another day."

"I think that's probably prudent."

"Yeah, well, all things considered, I feel pretty good."

"That's because you're on a morphine drip."

"I'd be much more comfortable at home."

"You'll survive another day in the hospital. You need anything?"

"I'm good right now. I just ordered lunch. Juliana Morgan stopped by to check on me. So, there's that."

I lifted an impressed brow. "Really?"

"Maybe I should get shot more often." I heard some commotion in the background. "I'll call you back. I gotta run. Dr. Parker is here."

He ended the call, and I slipped the phone back into my pocket.

Paris Delaney called a few minutes later.

"Did you get your interview?"

"I got a *'No comment.'* But I can still use the footage. And I got a call from a source who knows Simon and is familiar with his operation. Former employee. I'm going to meet them shortly. I'll let you know if that turns up anything interesting."

"Keep me posted."

"Quid pro quo, Deputy. Quid pro quo."

She hung up.

I strolled into the galley to make a sandwich. I spent the day taking it easy, doing research on the Internet about the Blue Rain. There was a lot of speculation online as to the thieves who had stolen the jewel, but nothing definitive.

It was the afternoon when I got a text on an encrypted messaging app with a video clip attached. I pressed play, and my heart sank. My jaw tightened, and my hands balled into fists.

Paris Delaney was blindfolded, bound, and gagged. She struggled and moaned, and mascara had stained her cheeks. The room was dark. Somebody stuck today's newspaper in front of the lens. It took a second for the camera to focus on the date.

The video was followed by a text: [Bring the diamond, or the reporter dies. Come alone. Tell no one, or she dies.]

GPS coordinates and a time were given. It was followed with another demand. [Send proof of the diamond.]

I didn't blame them for wanting proof. They'd gone through the trouble of kidnapping Paris, and they wanted to make sure I had something to trade for her. Though I knew this wouldn't be much of a trade.

Paris and I had our moments, and we didn't always see eye-to-eye. But I wasn't going to leave her high-and-dry.

I took a picture of the sparkling diamond and texted it back. [If anything happens to her, I will find you and kill you].

There was no reply.

I knew how these things worked. The only way they would let her go was if she couldn't ID them. And even then, I wasn't too sure they would keep their end of the bargain.

I immediately forwarded the video file to Isabella, then followed up with a call. "Analyze that video clip. See if you can extract any location data."

I filled her in on all the details.

Isabella's fingers frantically clacked against her keyboard. "Her phone isn't on the grid."

"What's the last location you have for her?"

"1172 Pelican Place. Looks like a small single-family home on the southeast side."

"She was going to meet a source."

"Well, it looks like that house is vacant."

"Where's Simon Brennan now?"

"You think he's responsible?"

"Positive."

Isabella's fingers danced across the keys again. "His phone is off-grid. What are you going to do?"

"Get her back."

60

Teal waves crashed against the bow as I plowed through the swells in the new wake boat, heading out to sea. The engine rumbled, leaving a frothy white wake. The boat pitched and rolled, and the wind blew through my hair.

I wore a bulletproof vest under my shirt. My pockets were loaded with extra magazines. I had an AR 15 on the deck near the console, and I had a few smoke and flash-bang grenades for good measure.

I was on my own. I was heading out in the middle of nowhere with no backup and not much of a plan. Probably not the smartest thing to do, but I didn't have much of a choice. If they heard a helicopter or saw patrol boats, it would be putting Paris at risk. And with a known leak in the department, I didn't trust anyone except for Daniels, JD, and Denise.

It took a half-hour to reach the destination. A sport boat waited with two masked thugs on board. Big muscle heads. I had no doubt it was Simon's newly hired henchmen.

I throttled back and let the boat drift on the swells, approaching the two goons. I palmed the diamond in my pocket, pulled it out, and held my fist over the gunwale as I approached, ready to drop the stone. I shouted across the water, "Where's Paris?"

"Hand over the diamond, and she will be released."

"Sorry. It doesn't work that way. I need to see her with my own eyes. And she goes first. Otherwise, this diamond goes to Davy Jones' Locker."

The two thugs exchanged a glance with each other.

They made a call, presumably to Simon.

After a brief back and forth with him, the thugs shouted back to me, "The diamond or the girl will die."

These guys would kill me as soon as I handed it over. "Trust is earned, gentlemen. I need to see that Paris is okay. We'll take it from there."

They relayed the message, and a moment later, one of the goons said, "Follow us."

He took the helm and cranked up the engine, and I followed them through the teal water. The sun angled toward the horizon, and the sky turned shades of pink and orange. Gulls drifted about on the breeze.

I followed them for another 15 minutes until we came upon *Mr. Sparkles*. There was horizon for as far as the eye could see. There wasn't another soul on the water within visual range.

Simon stood on the aft deck of the superyacht. He had Paris by the arm. Her hands were bound, and she was still blindfolded.

One of his newly hired thugs stood on the swim platform, chumming the water from a slop bucket.

I navigated the wake boat toward the stern and held the diamond over the water once again between my thumb and index finger so Simon could see it.

The boat rolled with the swells, and it wouldn't take too much for the jewel to slip from my fingers.

Simon shouted at me. "We could have done this the easy way, Deputy. But you had to make it complicated. Your friend hasn't seen my face. My associates wore masks. This could have been clean. I'll be honest. Now you're not walking away from this."

"Let Paris go, and you can have what you want."

He escorted Paris down to the swim platform. She awkwardly navigated the steps, not able to see.

Simon's goon kept chumming the water, and the growing sense of dread swelled within me. I could smell the rotten slop from here, and I knew the sharks could smell it for miles.

The two other goons hovered nearby on the sport boat.

I glanced below the surface of the clear water and could already see the toothy bastards circling.

"You want me to let her go? I'll let her go." Simon pushed Paris into the water. She splashed into the swells and frantically paddled to stay afloat, her wrists still bound. The commotion just attracted unwanted attention. The sharks were tuned to respond to fear and distress.

My whole body tensed. "Paris, swim to my voice!"

"The diamond," Simon demanded.

61

Paris managed to pull off the blindfold. I'm not sure that was such a good idea. She freaked out when she saw the sharks circling below. With bound wrists she paddled toward the wake boat.

I lobbed the precious gem in the air, hurling it toward Simon. I didn't care about the stone.

His goons opened fire.

Muzzle flash flickered from barrels, and bullets snapped through the air.

I ducked below the gunwale and drew my weapon.

The blue diamond glittered in the setting sun toward the aft deck of *Mr. Sparkles*.

I'll admit, I threw it a little short on purpose.

Simon reached for it and snatched it before it plunked into the water. A grin played on his face as he opened his palm and admired his new acquisition.

A swell rolled by, rocking *Mr. Sparkles,* setting Simon off balance. He bobbled the stone. It fell to the swim platform, dancing about. Simon bent over, trying to scoop it up before it disappeared forever, but it fell into the water and sank below. Simon lurched forward to grasp it and fell off the swim platform into the shark-infested water.

My pistol hammered against my palm, the deafening report echoing across the water. The smell of gunpowder filled my nostrils as I exchanged fire with the two goons on the sport boat.

The goon on the swim platform joined in the shooting gallery.

Bullets whizzed overhead, smacking into the fiberglass hull, shattering the windshield on the wake boat.

The brand-new wake boat!

I tossed a flash-bang grenade over the gunwale into the thug's speedboat.

BANG!

With the blinding flash and a deafening concussion, it dazed the two goons.

I continued firing in their direction.

One of my bullets caught a goon in the neck.

Blood spurted like a fountain.

He fell back, writhing on the deck.

I took aim at his comrade and fired a few more shots. With the rolling swells, it made accuracy difficult.

He fired back, and the bullet smacked the gunwale inches from me. I ducked as fiberglass splintered.

I angled my pistol over the gunwale again and returned two more shots, catching the dirtbag in the forehead. His head exploded like a watermelon.

I swung my barrel toward the swim platform of *Mr. Sparkles* and fired two more rounds. It caught Mr. Chum in the knee.

Bones and cartilage exploded.

He crumpled and fell into the water. The big bastard couldn't swim, and by the looks of things, it wasn't long before a shark decided to see what he tasted like.

Paris had reached the wake boat.

I leaned over the gunwale, grabbed her wrists, and hoisted her out of the water. I pulled her over onto the deck. She lay terrified, dripping wet. I untied her wrists, and she flung her arms around me and squeezed tight.

"Are you okay?" I asked.

She nodded, still trembling.

I looked her over, but everything seemed to be in the right place. Nothing was missing.

I moved back to the gunwale, looking for Simon. He thrashed about, foaming the water, arms flailing. The teal swells took on a deep shade of crimson as he fought the furious beasts. They were in a full-on frenzy, and it didn't take long before there wasn't much left of Simon or Mr. Chum.

My heart pounded, and my skin was alive with adrenaline. I holstered my pistol and moved back to Paris. We drifted on the swells.

"I guess I owe you one," she said.

"Maybe you should vet your sources a little better before you go visit them by yourself," I said.

"I suppose that would be wise." Her eyes lit up. "But I just got the greatest story of my career. This is going to make me a star."

I just sighed and shook my head. There was no deterring Paris's ambition.

"What about the diamond?" she asked.

"If you want to go down there and look for it, be my guest?"

62

I called Sheriff Daniels, and it didn't take long before the area swarmed with patrol boats and Coast Guard. Tango One pattered overhead. After the water had cleared of sharks, the dive team searched for and recovered the Blue Rain. The gem would be returned to its rightful owner. Paris wanted to make sure her news crew would be able to get footage of the precious stone before it was returned.

Never let a photo op go to waste.

I filled out after-action reports at the station, then stopped by the hospital to check on JD. I told him the story, and he was a little upset that he got left out of the action.

"I could have gone with you."

I laughed. "It was probably good that you sat this one out."

Paris Delaney appeared on the flatscreen for her segment during the evening news regaling the audience with her traumatic experience and heroic rescue. I had agreed to do an interview with her, and she planned a special spotlight series that would air over the next week, detailing the entire story.

Jack was bound and determined to perform with Wild Fury, which was scheduled to play at Sonic Temple tomorrow night. He wasn't going to let a pesky little thing like a gunshot wound derail the event. It meant too much to him, and for more than the obvious reasons, which I would find out the night of the show. A few glasses of whiskey would numb things just enough to get on stage, he figured.

He was discharged the next morning from the hospital, and I helped him get settled in at home. He moved around gingerly. He couldn't really lift his left arm over his head. Laughing, coughing, and of course, singing loud caused pain.

I hired roadies to load the gear in and out and set up. It was a luxury that the band could afford now. They were making enough to cover expenses from streaming revenue, performance fees, T-shirt sales, and other merchandise. It wasn't a huge amount of money, but enough. Even if they weren't making enough, I'd have paid for it out-of-pocket. Loading gear in and out sucks. The band needed to focus on one thing and one thing only—putting on the best shows possible.

We hung out at the bar before the show, watching the opening act as *Wild Fury* fans flooded the venue.

Jack's eyes lit up when he saw Juliana Morgan step through the door. I wasn't disappointed to see her either. She was with Cat.

JD rushed to greet them and escorted the two beauties our way. We found a high-top table near the bar. JD flagged down a waitress, and the girls ordered.

"I was thinking you weren't going to show," JD teased.

"When you were in the hospital, I told you I would come to your show. Besides, Cat forced me."

Cat smiled. "Wild Fury is the hottest ticket in town."

Juliana gave her a skeptical glance. Then admitted, "I have to say, I'm impressed that you're going through with the show so soon after the attack."

"The show must go on," JD said. "I can't let all these people down."

"I'm sure they would understand."

"Rain checks aren't always possible. Some people don't get to see tomorrow."

"You were almost one of those people," Juliana said.

JD dismissed it as rubbish. "I was never in any danger."

I held my tongue. We were in plenty of danger.

"I heard you had quite the adventure," Cat said to me.

"It's been an interesting few days."

JD spotted a woman and her teenage son at the door. The bouncer pointed at Jack.

"If you'll excuse me for a moment," he said. JD darted from the barstool and greeted the woman and her son. The kid was about 15, and he looked at Jack with starstruck eyes. He escorted them to the table and introduced us.

"This is Sharon and her son Nicholas."

Sharon was the one who'd written the letter that brought us both to tears.

Jack introduced Nicholas to the rest of the band. It was clear to see the kid idolized them.

Sharon watched the interaction, and her eyes misted. "It's so kind of Thrash to give Nicholas this moment. All he's talked about is getting the opportunity to meet Wild Fury."

Nicholas had been diagnosed with an inoperable brain tumor. They had tried everything, but the tumor kept growing. The future was uncertain, and they had decided to discontinue treatment. Nicholas wanted to enjoy what time he had left.

There wasn't a dry eye around as Sharon told us their saga.

63

The place was packed by the time *Wild Fury* took the stage. The lights swirled, and fog billowed from machines. JD muscled through the pain, prancing around like a true rockstar. The crowd roared and cheered. Dizzy's guitar growled, and Crash's bass boomed. Styxx thundered the beat from behind his candy-apple red drum set. A wall of sound hit the audience from massive speakers, and Nicholas watched the whole show from the side of the stage. He got the VIP treatment.

They finished their set and slipped offstage. The lights went down, and the audience cheered and clapped, stomping their feet for more. The venue rumbled.

After they'd made the crowd wait for a few moments, the band retook the stage for an encore. JD grabbed the microphone and shouted, "We've got a very special guest here tonight." He looked at Nicholas, standing on the side of the stage. Jack tried not to choke up, but his throat got tight. "He's our biggest fan, and he plays a little guitar. Would you please welcome to the stage, Nicholas!"

The crowd erupted, and Nicholas looked stunned. He pointed to himself and mouthed the words, "Me?"

JD nodded and waved him out. The kid rushed on stage, and Dizzy handed him his guitar and helped him get the strap around his shoulder.

Nicholas looked out over the crowd with awe and wonder.

"You told me you know every Wild Fury song," JD said. "What song do you want to play?"

Nicholas thought about it for a moment. "All I Need."

The crowd roared, and Styxx clicked off the beat.

Nicholas looked down at the fretboard and positioned his hand, then rocked out the guitar part like a professional.

The crowd hollered even louder.

The kid was a little stiff at first, but it only took him a few bars to loosen up and get into the groove.

Jack screamed the verse into the microphone. It wasn't long before Nicholas pranced around on stage like a rock god.

Crash moved beside him, and the duo did synchronized '80s guitar moves.

The crowd ate it up.

Nicholas played three songs with the band before they called it a night.

I'm not sure to whom it meant more, JD or Nicholas.

64

J ack and the band said goodbye to Nicholas and wished him well. We headed back for the usual after-party on the *Avventura*. Cat convinced Juliana to come along. She was warming up to JD.

There were plenty of topless groupies frolicking in the Jacuzzi and sauntering around the sky deck.

"I can see why the Kappa's made you all honorary brothers," Juliana said.

"We have a little fraternity of our own," Jack replied.

He was pretty wrecked from his performance, so he found a comfortable spot and talked with Juliana for the rest of the evening, attempting to work his magic.

It didn't take long for Cat and me to adjourn to my stateroom, where we worked out the urge that had been sparked the first time we saw each other at *Gingerbread's*. She definitely liked to live life to the fullest.

It was a few days later when Professor Matthews went missing.

Not long after, a video was released online from an anonymous account. The professor's face was battered and bruised. His nose had been broken and now had a crooked angle. He had dark circles under his eyes that were multiple shades of purple, blue, yellow, and green. His face was speckled with cuts and abrasions. His lip was split, and what was once pristine hair was now matted and tousled. He had that hollow, terrified look of a man that had been tortured and abused. He read from a prepared statement admitting his crimes, taking responsibility for the campus rapes and murder, as well as the alleged sexual misconduct with students.

The video went viral, and all of the news channels picked it up.

A day later, he was released by his captors, and he walked into the Sheriff's Office and surrendered himself. He made a full confession. I had no doubt that his captors had threatened him with more torture and even death if he didn't comply.

An investigation was opened into his abduction and torture, but I don't think anybody pursued it with any real vigor. My guess was that his former victims banded together, perhaps their boyfriends, and carried out the kidnapping. Their version of vigilante justice. Who knows?

JD took it easy the next few weeks. We lounged around, fished, and searched for treasure. Jack convinced Juliana to go on a date with him, and he seemed to be melting her ice shield.

I had a few more dalliances with Cat.

Scuba divers discovered the body of a young man tied to an anchor not far from one of the reefs. The body was pretty decomposed and picked over by the critters of the sea—an all-you-can-eat buffet. Brenda was able to match dental records and ID the victim as Owen Ferguson. It didn't come as much of a surprise, given what he was tied to—a custom engraved anchor with the name of the boat, the *Man of Steel,* which happened to belong to the billionaire Flynn Westwood. In his haste to dump the body, Flynn had forgotten about the identifying markings. In the end, his vanity is what put him behind bars.

We served a warrant and arrested him. In the interrogation room, he said, "It was an accident. You have to believe me."

"Owen just accidentally got tied around an anchor," I said flatly.

"I panicked. I didn't know what to do." Flynn paused. "Owen found out I was sleeping with his girlfriend. We had all been drinking heavily. Owen pulled out a gun and threatened to kill me. We struggled, and the gun went off." His eyes filled. "There was so much blood."

"So you panicked. You cleaned up the mess, tied the rope around him, and tossed him overboard."

He nodded. "You believe me, don't you?"

"It doesn't matter what I believe. You'll have to convince a jury."

Scarlett came into town the day after Jack's Sonic Temple show and stayed for Thanksgiving. JD catered the feast, and we had a gathering aboard the *Avventura.* It was a time to come together with gratitude. Sheriff Daniels and the guys from the department attended. Denise was there, as well as Paris Delaney andTeagan. The usual suspects. We filled our bellies with smoked turkey and all the fixings and plenty of pumpkin pie. All was right with the world—until a few days later when Daniels called.

Ready for more?

The adventure continues with Wild Lights!

Join my newsletter and find out what happens next!

AUTHOR'S NOTE

Thanks for all the great reviews!

I've got more adventures for Tyson and JD. Stay tuned.

If you liked this book, let me know with a review on Amazon.

Thanks for reading!

—*Tripp*

TYSON WILD

Wild Ocean

Wild Justice

Wild Rivera

Wild Tide

Wild Rain

Wild Captive

Wild Killer

Wild Honor

Wild Gold

Wild Case

Wild Crown

Wild Break

Wild Fury

Wild Surge

Wild Impact

Wild L.A.

Wild High

Wild Abyss

Wild Life

Wild Spirit

Wild Thunder

Wild Season

Wild Rage

Wild Heart

Wild Spring

Wild Outlaw

Wild Revenge

Wild Secret

Wild Envy

Wild Surf

Wild Venom

Wild Island

Wild Demon

Wild Blue

Wild Lights

Wild...

CONNECT WITH ME

I'm just a geek who loves to write. Follow me on Facebook.

TRIPP ELLIS

www.trippellis.com

Made in United States
North Haven, CT
08 November 2021

10943477R00182